Naughty List

NAUGHTY OR NICE
BOOK ONE

CAMERON ALLIE

CAMERON
ALLIE

Chapter One

"Can I tell you something that's a little embarrassing for me?" Kylie sat on her friend's sofa, sipping hot cocoa while watching *Love Actually*. In the next room, the freshly decorated Christmas tree was twinkling brightly.

Kylie had met Hannah at work a few months ago, and they'd instantly hit it off. They were both single, both thirty years old, both personal trainers, and both on their second career after failing to enjoy what they'd initially set out to do.

Hannah had gone to college to become a social worker, but she had underestimated the emotional drain that came with such a demanding job. She'd burned out very quickly. Kylie had become a daycare teacher but quickly became frustrated with the broken system and quit after her first year.

As the holidays drew closer, Hannah had invited Kylie over to trim the tree and partake in some traditional holiday merriment. With the tree finished, a batch of gingerbread in the oven, and their bellies full of hot chocolate, they were both pretty tuckered out, and yet, tomorrow, they had plans to go shopping.

"Of course." Hannah glanced over but turned back to the screen.

Kylie thought Hannah's divided attention might make her confession easier to deliver. "I've never enjoyed sex."

"What?" Turning so fast she nearly spilled her mug, Hannah grabbed the remote, paused the film, and set down her cup. "What do you mean, you've never enjoyed sex?"

Kylie shrugged. "I don't know. It's always been just okay. Like I could take or leave it. It's something I should do because, well, that's what you do in a relationship, right?"

Hannah frowned. She didn't understand. Disappointed, Kylie wanted to disappear into the couch. She wished she hadn't said anything.

"Maybe you haven't been with the right guy?" she suggested.

"I've been with my fair share of men. None of them seem to do it for me." She didn't consider herself a floozy, but after a long-term relationship, a few shorter ones, and a couple of one-night stands, she knew sex was just a big disappointment for her.

"Maybe you're just not into sex. Some people aren't. Maybe you're asexual. Do you have sex with yourself?"

Kylie blushed. She really shouldn't have started this conversation.

When she didn't answer, Hannah brazenly went on. "Like, do you own any toys or touch yourself? Stuff like that?"

"I shouldn't have brought it up." Kylie went to pick up the remote to unpause the film, but Hannah snatched it from her.

"No. This is important." Hannah switched the TV off. "You know I won't judge you, right? You can tell me anything."

Kylie wasn't sure. Their friendship was so new, but they'd bonded very fast. Kylie felt closer to Hannah than she did to any of her friends from high school. At times, she even felt closer to her than she felt to her own sister.

"How about I tell you something first? Something I don't normally share. Will that help?"

Kylie stretched forward and set her mug down on the coffee table. "Look, Hannah, I don't want to push you—"

"I visit a BDSM club," Hannah announced. "You know what that is?"

With wide eyes, Kylie nodded.

"I visit a BDSM club, and recently, I've been holding the attention of two Doms. Do you understand?"

"Sort of."

"Sometimes, I have sex with both of them. They tell me what to do, and I do it. No questions asked."

Kylie's heart started to race. Maybe she could open up to Hannah. Her lifestyle brushed up against the things Kylie had often fantasized about trying but had never acted on. Two Doms, though, that wasn't for her. She just wanted one good sexual experience. Was that too much to ask for for Christmas?

"So, that's my little secret. How about you? Do you have sex with yourself?" Hannah circled back to her original question, leaving Kylie with a million questions she wanted to ask but didn't dare to.

Bravely, she replied, "Yes."

"So you think you would enjoy sex? You know, with the right partner?"

She nodded.

"Are you gay?"

Kylie shook her head. "No! Not that there's anything wrong with that, but I'm just not."

"Okay. So maybe it's the guys you've been seeing. What are they like?"

They'd all been jerks. Well, not all of them, but most. "They're either really boring or selfish assholes in bed."

Hannah pursed her lips.

As she thought about it, Kylie wrung her hands. "Can you tell me more about the BDSM club?"

Slowly, a grin came over Hannah's mouth. "Got a little fantasy tucked away in there?"

Kylie felt her face go red again. "Maybe."

"So the club I go to is kind of like a nightclub. There's a bar, some dancing, a main stage for exhibitionists, but there are also private rooms. There's a dungeon master to ensure everything is safe and consensual. And when it comes to alcohol, there are strict rules, particularly for those engaging in active play."

"But what goes on there?" Kylie didn't want to be nosy, but she was curious. She wondered what active play was.

"Some people go to hook up or act out a scene. Some go to meet new people or show off their subs. There are all types of fetishes, though admittedly, this club isn't as hardcore as others I've been to. This one is a little more vanilla, but it's not uncommon to see a good whipping or paddling. What are you into?"

Kylie bit her lip as she considered telling Hannah. "I've read all the books."

Hannah rolled her eyes. "You mean like that Grey book?"

Clearly, that wasn't impressive. Everyone and their mother, hell, their grandmother, had read about Christian Grey.

Kylie gave her a little more. "I've read Tiffany Reisz, Anne Rice, Sierra Cartwright, Joey W. Hill, Angela Knight, and Angel Payne. To name a few."

"Okay. There's something there to work with."

Briefly closing her eyes, Kylie fessed up. "I've watched a lot of videos too." Her blush deepened as she glanced at her friend. "And I've joined a couple of online chats, but nothing ever face-to-face or via video. Only messaging."

"Now we're talking." Hannah laughed. "So it's more than just a passing interest."

"Yes," Kylie admitted. "I never knew how to get into the scene. I kept dating assertive men, assholes really, but it's just led to disappointing sex."

"Well, yeah. If you're interested in a fetish when it comes to sex, you're not going to find it with some vanilla man."

Or one that was entirely too concerned with his own pleasure to even care if she had an orgasm or not.

"It sounds like you're a submissive, or want to be, if I'm reading the situation correctly."

"I guess so." Yes, yes, that's what she wanted.

Suddenly, Hannah's expression lit up, and she began clapping her hands. "Maybe we can get you laid by Santa! It sounds like that's exactly what you need!"

Not understanding at all what she was talking about, Kylie frowned. "What?"

"Each December at the club, this guy comes in dressed like Santa." Hannah excitedly patted her arm. "He's hot as sin. Chiseled body, gorgeous face, cocky attitude galore. He comes in wearing a Santa hat and pants. Sometimes the jacket and suspenders too. He's quite the Christmas treat."

Kylie imagined what Hannah described and wasn't disappointed by the fantasy that crossed her mind, being pulled across his lap for a hearty spanking.

"At the club, he doesn't do much but hold court."

"What does that mean?" Kylie wrinkled her nose.

"He orders a few drinks, takes in the scenes, and chats up the women. He might give a few kisses, an occasional stroke, and a couple of spankings here and there. I think he's fingered a few subs, but he pretty much waits until right before Christmas."

Kylie realized she was leaning forward in her seat. It was also when she realized her panties were wet. "Then what?"

"He picks one lucky sub to take home on Christmas Eve eve."

"Really?"

"Yep. He could have a different woman each night, but he doesn't. He waits and looks for the perfect addition to his naughty list."

Kylie swatted at her. "You're making that up!"

"I am not!" Hannah laughed. "Last year, I tried to get on the naughty list, but he didn't pick me. That's okay though, because I found Darrell and Derek. But we should get you on Santa's naughty list."

Kylie wasn't so sure. Sex with some random stranger? And kinky sex at that. What if she didn't like it? What if she didn't like him? "Who is he?"

Hannah shrugged. "No one seems to know who he is. He just randomly showed up about seven years ago, apparently. He never gives his real name. The theory is that he's not from around here but comes every December for the holidays. Maybe to visit family. But Kylie, every woman he picks comes back to the club in the

New Year and goes on and on about how great he was. Like, they won't shut up about it. For months."

Kylie shrugged. What did she have to lose? He might not even pick her. Going to the club with Hannah might prove to be what she needed. Maybe she'd meet a Dom who made her swoon, or more correctly, kneel. Perhaps she'd find a remarkable man to introduce her to the lifestyle. She could find out if that was what her sex life had been missing. It was worth a try.

"I'm going on Thursday night for drinks with the guys before we go back to Darrell's place. Do you want to come with us?"

It was now or never. Take one little risk. No one needed to know about it aside from Hannah. One little gamble that could get her everything she wanted. Swallowing her fear, she replied, "I wouldn't know what to wear."

"We're going shopping tomorrow, right?" Hannah took a sip of her hot chocolate. "Now, we've just got to add a couple more stops."

After a busy day of shopping with Hannah, it took Kylie three trips from the car to bring all her packages into the house. She lived with her brother and sister in a house they'd purchased together.

"What did you get me?" Her sister, Janet, asked as she started peeking into the bags.

"Don't look!" Kylie shouted and snatched away the bag she was looking in. Janet was a notorious snoop, and this year, Kylie had two reasons to keep her shopping bags secret. Sure, Janet's gift was in one; she'd gotten her a nice sweater and some of her favorite chocolates. But it was another bag she didn't want her sister's nose in. Actually, it was several bags with new clothing and toys for herself. Maybe she'd gone a little overboard, but liberation had felt so good.

While removing her boots and coat, she kept an eye on Janet, knowing she'd poke her fingers into whichever bag was closest.

With her hands behind her back, Janet rocked on her heels and looked so much like a child trying desperately to behave despite her naughty impulses. "So, did you finish your Christmas shopping?"

"No," she lied. She had to, or Janet would keep looking until she found her gift. In an attempt to distract her, she asked, "Whose car is out front?"

"Freddie's."

Freddie was their brother's friend from back when they used to play hockey together. Her brother had gone on to become a doctor —a gynecologist. And Freddie had used his interest in computers and his artistry skills to develop his own video game. From there, he'd created a video game company. Now, he had a small empire. His company had its fingers in multiple pies. Freddie rarely did much of the creating when it came to the games now. Instead, all his time was dedicated to running the business.

"It's a new car."

"You know Freddie." Janet shrugged. "He never keeps anything for long. Do you need help carrying this up?"

She laughed at her sister's last effort to snoop. "Nope."

Both she and her brother had a locked chest in their closets where they kept the things they didn't want Janet to find. Several bags would be going in it this year. She started with those. Grabbing particular bags, she left behind the ones holding gifts for her parents, brother, and friends.

A few of the lingerie pieces she'd selected from Victoria's Secret, she hung in the closet, but the risqué corset and new vibrator, arousal cream, and Kegel balls, she put in the chest. Janet's Christmas gift got shoved into the wooden box, as well. She locked the chest and returned to the main floor for the rest of the gifts.

After finally getting things settled into her room, she headed back downstairs. It would be a long wait until Thursday night. She'd spent the day asking Hannah questions and trying on sexy new outfits. Things she could mix and match. She felt much better about her decision to visit the club and was anxious to get her first peek at what it would be like inside.

Heading to the kitchen for a drink, she grabbed a glass from the cupboard and filled it with water and ice from the dispenser in the fridge.

"Merry Christmas."

Bracing herself, she turned toward the voice with a smile on her face. "Merry Christmas, Freddie." She always had to brace herself for the sight of him. He was breathtaking with his deep green eyes, golden-brown hair, and movie-star good looks. His smile made her weak in the knees, and he was super nice to boot. One of the sweetest men she'd ever met.

Maybe too sweet.

Years ago, when they were still in high school, he'd hinted at asking her out, but she'd shut that down fast. Despite his good looks, winning personality, and charming disposition, he just didn't do it for her. He was too nice. He didn't have that alpha-male quality she was so sexually attracted to.

Of course, after the death of his parents, he hadn't shown any interest in her, or any other girl for that matter. He'd been swallowed in grief.

"We're looking for a fourth for cards," he told her. She glanced past him to the dining room where her brother and sister sat chatting at the table. "Would you like to play?"

She shrugged. "Sure."

Freddie refilled his own glass with water and nodded to her outfit. "That's a cute sweater. Is it new?"

And that's what she meant by too sweet. He was genuinely interested in her appearance, and he had no interest in getting beneath the sweater. Most of her brother's friends would have called it hot or sexy. They would have ogled her breasts or stood a little too close. But not Freddie. He was a gentleman.

"It's new-ish."

With his glass, he motioned to her waist. "I like this belt thing."

For decorative purposes, a brown belt hung loosely around her hips. Kylie played with the end of it. "Thanks."

"Did you manage to get your shopping done? I know you like

to get it done early, and X said you were out shopping today," he said, referencing her brother, Xavier.

"I did, but don't tell Janet," Kylie whispered as they approached the dining room.

"Your secret is safe with me, though I assume she already knows you're done. She's like a bloodhound when it comes to surprises and gifts."

"Probably. Good thing I've got it locked away already." She took a sip of her water. "Do you have much shopping to do?"

"Just your brother and my aunt."

She smiled at him. "So...you haven't started yet?"

"No. I suppose not." He laughed. "Any hints on what your brother might want for Christmas?"

"I don't know. I got him a couple of new shirts to wear to the office, but you and I aren't exactly on the same playing field when it comes to gifts. I mean, last year you got him a Switch and like every possible accessory and game to go with it."

"All three of you love playing it, don't you?"

"Oh, of course we do, but that's not my point. You could have bought him an awful lot of sweaters for that amount."

He chuckled at her joke. "I'm thinking about flying him out to Vegas with me to test drive a Porsche GT3 RS. Do you think he'd be into that?"

"Oh, for sure. He'd love that!"

"I thought so." He nudged her with his elbow. "And the best part is I won't have to set foot in a store to get it."

Kylie laughed. She was sure the best part would be spending time with his friend and experiencing something so rare and unique, but she didn't doubt that staying away from stores during Christmas was a bonus.

They played cards for a few hours, and after dinner, Freddie stayed to join them for a couple of rounds of Mario Cart on the Switch, but Kylie excused herself. She was anxious to test out a few of her new toys. On her iPad, she downloaded a new erotica and, part way through, found herself unlocking the chest in her room.

Thursday night couldn't come fast enough.

Chapter Two

Kylie felt awkward as she removed her long winter coat and left it in the coat room. In a way, Thursday night had come both far too quickly and yet not fast enough. Finally, she was at the club.

Next to her, Hannah stood in a long white shirt synched at the waist by a corset that didn't cover her breasts, so they were only covered by the thin white shirt. Thigh-high boots added a couple of inches to her already tall height, and her hair was pulled up in a high ponytail. She explained to Kylie that ordinarily, she'd be wearing a lot less clothing, but as she was coming with a newbie, she didn't want to make her friend uncomfortable. Apparently, she'd had to ask her Doms for permission before selecting the outfit.

Kylie was starting to doubt her decision to come. Did she really want to be told what to do? To be told how to dress?

On the way out of the coatroom, they passed a woman wearing nothing but a harness and being led around on a leash.

Maybe this had been a mistake.

"Come on." Hannah grabbed Kylie's hand and began leading her through the club. She must have sensed her hesitation because she told her, "Everything will be fine. No one will make you do anything you don't want to do."

"Okay." Putting on a brave face, Kylie followed along. It was very much like a nightclub. Flashing lights, thudding music—though rock rather than dance blared through the speakers—and an active bar and a dance scene. Booths, tables, and a dancefloor filled up most of the space. The main difference was people's attire: dark clothing, leather, latex, or, in some cases, a complete lack of clothing. Some people wore only harnesses or nipple clamps. She'd even spotted a few cock cages.

She tried not to stare. Reading about it or watching porn was one thing, but seeing it live was something completely different. She was a newbie, as Hannah had said, but she didn't have to act like one, so she attempted not to gawk at everyone.

Hannah escorted her to a booth where two men already sat there, waiting for them, it seemed.

Darrell and Derek, she assumed. Both wore tight black denim jeans, but one wore a black dress shirt, only partly buttoned, and the other wore a black mesh top. As she approached, she could feel their gaze on her body.

Feeling embarrassed, she hoped Hannah's clothing choices for her had been appropriate. The heels were a little awkward to walk in, but somehow, she was managing.

When they reached the table, Hannah spun her around. "What do you think?"

More so than before, their gazes combed over her. She felt them linger on her breasts, her thighs, her legs. Just like Hannah, Kylie wore thigh-high boots laced up the sides. Fashionably ripped tights covered the rest of her legs before disappearing beneath a black and purple miniskirt. The corset was a vintage gothic style, with swing hooks up the front rather than buttons. A chunky black belt crossed over the bottom. On her wrists, she wore leather cuff bracelets.

"I approve," the dark-haired man wearing the dress shirt replied, giving them a thumbs up.

The blond continued to leer at her. "Definitely hot. She'll be a hit."

"Thank you, Sirs," Hannah replied as though they were complimenting her own body. She helped Kylie into the booth, urging her to sit next to the blond before she squished in next to her. "This is Darrell." She pointed to the blond in the mesh top before swinging her finger toward the other man. "And Derek."

"It's lovely to meet you."

Derek laughed. "I wouldn't be so sure."

Confused, Kylie looked to her friend.

Hannah giggled. "You're new and unsure if this is the place for you. You might be a little shocked at some of the things you see happen tonight."

"Exactly." Darrell reached out and stroked a strand of her hair. His smile was kind, and when his finger grazed the exposed skin of her shoulder, her heart beat a little faster.

"We're going to get you ladies something to drink. Then we'll dance," Derek informed them as though he was the authority on their activities for the evening. Kylie supposed he would be.

Kylie and Hannah stretched out in the booth as the men left with their drink orders. Kylie's gaze followed them as they approached the bar. "They don't expect me to join you guys, do they?"

"No." Hannah shook her head. "They know I don't want to share them. But that might not stop them from touching and teasing you a bit. Will that be a problem?"

Kylie touched her hair in the place where Darrell had touched her. "I'm not sure."

"If it is, just tell them, and they'll back off. Derek doesn't normally like to dance. Normally, he watches while Darrell and I dance. Actually, he likes to watch a lot of things Darrell and I do together." Hannah's laugh was rich, and Kylie didn't know if she was joking. "But if he's interested in dancing tonight, it might mean one of them will want to dance with you."

"Oh, I think I can handle that," she paused, "but what about the Santa?"

"I thought we'd have a drink and dance a bit first before I take you to see him. Right now, you're pretty rigid. You need to loosen up a bit first. Besides, he always has a long line-up of girls at the beginning of the night."

She said that as though he feasted on them. What did he do with them?

Kylie deflated with Hannah's words. She'd been trying hard to relax, but it wasn't showing. Maybe a rum and Coke would help. Shortly after the Doms returned, they began conversing over their beverages. It eased Kylie's mind when they chatted about work and family rather than the dirty things they did with Hannah.

It turned out Darrell was a financial advisor for a local bank, and Derek was a nurse in a local children's hospital. They asked where Kylie worked and if she had any siblings. They talked about holiday traditions and whether they liked eggnog or not. Darrell was Jewish, so he told her all about his customs, which fascinated her and made her mouth water with talk of all the delicious foods he consumed over Hanukkah.

After her second drink, she began to feel more comfortable and agreed to let them take her onto the dancefloor.

Hannah had been right. They did want to dance with her. Mostly, it was Darrell's hands wrapped around her waist while Derek held Hannah close, grinding on her body, kissing her, and Kylie was pretty sure she'd occasionally seen him squeeze her breasts or pinch her nipples through the shirt she wore.

As she watched them, feeling Darrell's hands on her body, seeing the other bodies writhing on the dancefloor had turned her on. At one point, a demonstration started on the stage where a man whipped a woman until she orgasmed. Kylie had tried not to stare, but Darrell had seemed to note her interest and had ensured she was facing the stage no matter how they were dancing.

After the stage went dark, Hannah approached her. "Let's introduce you to Santa." She grabbed her hand and pulled her from the dance floor. "Apparently, this outfit has got Derek all hot and bothered. He's got some Roman slave girl fantasy he wants to play out, and now I'm as eager as him."

Kylie smirked. The night had become lots of fun. Whether things worked out with Santa or not, she'd at least had a good time, and she felt confident enough that she'd be able to come back to the club.

"So let's get you to Santa because Derek hates to wait."

"Where is he?" Even though she'd been searching for him all evening, she'd yet to spot Santa.

Motioning, Hannah said, "Normally, he's in one of the back booths."

As they neared the back of the room, Kylie caught a glimpse of red, but she still couldn't see past the group of women crushed around him.

They pushed through the crowd, and sure enough, there he was. Santa.

Bare-chested, he sat on the bench with one hand wrapped around a beer bottle and the other resting on the hip of the scantily clad woman on his lap. He was a gorgeous specimen in red pants trimmed with white faux fur and a Santa hat sitting crookedly on his head.

One she'd seen before.

"See, he literally has a line-up." Hannah pointed. "It's some serious competition."

Three women stood in line like kids at the mall, waiting for their chance on his lap. But they didn't interest Kylie. Not when the man himself was so intriguing. Not when Santa had been in her kitchen that very weekend. And especially not when he was a man she'd grown up knowing.

"That's Freddie," she stated dumbly, as though Hannah had no idea who she was talking about.

Kylie squinted, not quite believing that it could be. Not after everything Hannah had told her about Santa. It just didn't line up with the man she knew. If not for a few photos she'd seen of Freddie at various charity events where he showed up with a random model or actress on his arm, she would have suspected he was still a virgin. Not someone capable of dominating a woman in the bedroom.

"Who's Freddie?"

"The Santa." Kylie motioned to him. "He's a friend of my brother's."

Hannah's eyes went wide. "Seriously?"

"At least, I think it is." She stared at him until he noticed her. His eyes narrowed in recognition. He paused, strained to see her better, his gaze dipping down her body. Finally, he turned away. It seemed as though he'd dismissed the possibility that he knew her, but his reaction only solidified her opinion. It was Freddie. "No, I'm sure it's him."

"Oh, this will be even better than I thought!"

"What?" Kylie tried to stop Hannah from dragging her toward the line. "I can't go now."

"You have to!"

"No way!" Kylie tried to stop her friend from tugging her toward the back of the line. "I'm too embarrassed."

"If something as simple as this embarrasses you, then maybe you don't belong here." Hannah dropped her arm.

Kylie chewed the inside of her cheek as she joined the back of the line. "I don't know."

"He's hot enough to melt the snow, and you've got a better chance than anyone else here if he does know you."

"But what you don't know about him is he's a really nice guy," Kylie whispered.

"So?"

"So how can he be a Dom?"

"Just because he's dominant in the bedroom or dungeon or whatever doesn't mean he has to be some asshole in everyday life."

She tried not to shuffle her feet. She snuck another peek at him. It just didn't make any sense. Did her brother know about Freddie's secret lifestyle?

She doubted it.

He caught her gaze again. This time, he held it longer, scrutinizing her. Turning his attention back to the brunette on his lap, he cupped her nape and treated her to a long, deep kiss, which seemed to leave her dazed. Kylie felt odd watching the intimate act, almost like she was watching one of her soft-core porns. After everything she'd seen tonight, watching Freddie kiss the woman somehow made Kylie uncomfortable.

She couldn't be jealous, though. Right?

When he let the woman up for air, he nudged her off his lap, looked again toward Kylie, and then motioned with one finger for her to come closer.

"You're up, slugger." Hannah pushed her past the other women waiting in line.

She'd been comfortable in her boots after dancing in them for a while, but suddenly, she found herself focusing on each step, trying not to trip. When she stood in front of him, his gaze bore into her.

"Leave us." He motioned for the rest of the women to disband from the line. They dispersed quickly, a few grumbling as they left.

His stare traveled down her body, lingering on the swell of her breasts above the corset, the flare of her hips, and her high heels. For the first time ever, she felt objectified by Freddie. His interest, while not clear on his face, was evident in his gaze.

While he sat back in his booth, his stare returned to her face; this time, a slight smile played on his lips. "It is you."

Chapter Three

"Yep. It's me." Somehow, she kept her voice from trembling.

He tapped his thigh, indicating she should sit. Debating her choices, Kylie stared at his lap.

"I won't bite," he teased. "At least not tonight." When she still didn't move, he continued, "I also won't ask a second time."

Blinking at the dominance in his tone, Kylie slowly approached him, turned, and placed herself on his lap. With her legs hooked over his, she sat stiffly, attempting not to touch him more than she had to. "I can't believe you're the Santa."

"I can't believe you're here. You've never been here before."

Surely, he meant during Christmas when he was at the club. He couldn't possibly know she was a virgin to the BDSM scene, right?

"I don't get it," she told him. "I just can't consolidate Freddie, my brother's nicer than nice, sweeter than candy best friend, with the man who promises women they'll have the night of their lives in his pleasure chamber."

Freddie grinned. "You can't, huh?"

She shook her head.

"So you've never thought of me that way before?" He leaned closer, his breath against her ear. "You know, sexually."

Sucking in a breath, she shook her head again.

"Shame." He tsked. "I think of you that way often."

Her eyes widened. "You do?"

"Oh, all the time." His fingers slipped beneath the edge of her skirt, tracing a hot line along her thigh.

Trying to contain her nervous energy, Kylie laughed. "No, you don't." She was sure of it. His gaze never lingered, and he never made inappropriate comments or suggestions. There was no way he'd been able to hide an attraction to her.

"Oh, I do." His hand traveled a little higher. "You just haven't been paying attention."

She glared. "I think I would have noticed."

"Evidently not."

It was pointless to argue with him. Suddenly, she was beginning to see the divide. Freddie wouldn't have argued, and he certainly wouldn't have stated his opinion with sure finality.

Was he really this dominant Santa? She had to know the truth. If she was going to risk offering herself in ways she never had before, she needed to know he was the real deal. "I still don't think you're the Santa. This is some kind of game, right? A joke on me?"

"No joke." He reclined in the booth, his hand still possessively on her thigh. "Women come here and tell me their wildest fantasies and hope I'll make them come true."

"Apparently, you do a good job of it." Kylie glanced around at the women who hovered nearby, hoping to rejoin him.

"Why are you here, Kylie? I don't think you frequent these types of places. This must be a first for you."

She refused to answer that without first getting some insurance. She had to know for sure that he really was who he claimed to be. "I don't believe those women told you anything dirty for a second. You're not the Santa."

Freddie shook his head with a sigh. "You have so little faith in me. You really can't believe women find me alluring? Sexy even?"

"Oh, I do not doubt that." She could feel the heat of his bare chest. He was sexy. She'd always found him attractive, but that wasn't what she had an issue with. "You're too nice to be a Dom. Make me a believer."

That sexy smile of his returned as though her challenge pleased him. Leaning closer, his forehead nearly brushing hers, he looked toward a woman across the room sitting at the bar. "That one wants me to stuff a vibrator in her pussy, lock her in a cage, leave her for a few hours until she can barely walk, then fuck her until the sun comes up and she can't move, much less beg for more."

Kylie's face got hot, and she felt her pussy clench at the scene he'd depicted. Maybe she was in over her head. She hadn't expected him to utter any of those words. Had they really come from Freddie's mouth?

"That one," he said, motioning with his head to a red-haired woman nearby. "She wants me to strip her naked, come all over her. On her tits, her stomach, her pussy. Then she wants me to take pictures of my artwork."

She squirmed a bit. Would he do that? Take pictures of his partner? Would he take photos of *her*? Would she be okay with that?

His fingers dug into her flesh, making her remember this was more than just a game she was playing. If Hannah was right, she had a better chance of gaining his attention than any of the other ladies here. If that was true, there was no backing out now.

But wasn't that what she wanted? Someone she could trust her body to? Someone with the skill and knowledge to give her mind-blowing sex. Was Freddie that person? Had he been all along?

He was so close she could smell his aftershave, could see how beautiful his lips were. She could feel his hard thighs beneath hers.

Lastly, he nodded toward the brunette that had been on his lap when she approached. "That one's partner is bisexual and she's into voyeurism. She wants me to fuck her sub while he eats her out."

Kylie squirmed again. She couldn't help it, not with the way her wet panties were rubbing against her. This time, she had to ask, "Would you do that?"

"*That?*" he asked, prompting her to say the words.

She hesitated. "Have anal?"

"I have. Not with a man, though." He clarified, "Nothing

wrong with that, of course, but I'm into women. And yes, I've taken several subs that way before." His hand slid a little further up her skirt, so far up that he was practically grabbing her hip. "I think it's hot."

Kylie couldn't help how enflamed her face was. He'd shocked her with the things he'd said, and, in the process, he'd convinced her that he was not only the Santa Dom but that he was also capable of doing the things she needed. Already she was wet and trying desperately not to rub herself against him like a bitch in heat.

His hand came out from beneath her skirt, and he put some distance between them. "Now, tell me, little one, why are you here?"

Glancing up at him, she chewed her lip. She was as innocent as he'd presumed, as inexperienced as any vanilla woman itching for things she'd read about, itching for a firm hand and a stern tone. But she hadn't known how or who to ask for it.

Looking at him, she realized she wanted those things from Freddie. Maybe it would be better if her first time submitting was to a Dom was with someone she knew—someone who would make her feel at ease and slowly introduce her to the lifestyle.

Freddie would definitely do that.

"You were right. This is my first time." She traced a line down those firm abs, a little in awe of how solid they were. She made sure her gaze was direct, as she wanted to shock him as much as he'd shocked her. Gathering all her courage, she said the words she'd so often thought to herself but had never been able to admit to anyone. "I want to be fucked, hard. To be used up. To be completely spent and at a man's total mercy."

His mouth curved into a smile. "Then I think you've come to the right place."

Releasing a breath, she relaxed. Thank God. If she were lucky, he wouldn't make her wait until December twenty-third.

He pointed around the room. "Any of these Doms would be happy to accommodate you, I'm sure."

Wait a minute, was he just going to brush her aside, after her confession? She frowned. "I don't want them."

He cocked his head to the side. "You don't?"

"No."

"Then what is it you want?"

"To get on your naughty list."

"Are you sure about that?" His hand returned to her leg, coasting up her thigh, this time between her legs. She held her breath.

She nodded vigorously. "That's why I came here. To meet Santa and get on his naughty list."

"And you still want that, even though it's me?"

She blinked. His hand was lingering between her thighs, not moving, just there, warm and big. She wanted to rock her hips forward, wanted him to slide it up further. "I want it more than ever."

His free hand cupped her chin. For a moment, she thought he might kiss her, and she wasn't entirely sure how she felt about that. She was eager for a taste, but not ten minutes ago, he'd had his tongue in another woman's mouth, and who knew how many women's mouths before that?

But rather than lean toward her, his stare turned hard and mean. "You need to know, Kylie, this isn't some game. Something for you to do to pass the time, to experiment with and walk away from just because you feel like it. If you want to be on my naughty list, I'm going to test you. I will ask you to do things that push against your boundaries." His light touch evolved into a firm grip. "To get on my naughty list, you must be just that. Naughty. You have to do every dirty, filthy thing I ask."

Her pulse spiked. Was this what she truly wanted? Her brain screamed at her, telling her no, but her body strained toward him. Her nipples tightened, and her pussy throbbed at all the wicked possibilities.

"Do you understand? Are you willing to make those types of sacrifices? Your pride? Your humility?"

She exhaled. "Yes."

"Think you can do what I ask of you? No hesitation, no questioning my commands?"

Nodding, she agreed.

"Good." He brushed his lips against her ear. "I want you to start thinking about me. About all the things I'm going to make you do. About my cock shoved deep inside you. About you dripping wet and begging me to fuck you."

She shook with need.

His hands tightened on her. She could feel his fingers digging into her thigh. "Don't move."

Her body went rigid at his order.

"Think about all those limits I'm going to push. Think about all the ways you're going to please me, Kylie: with your mouth, your tits, your cunt. Because come the twenty-third, I'm taking someone home with me, and if you're not at the top of the naughty list, it might very well be someone else."

"Wait. What?" She broke free from his grip and turned her stare on him.

He raised an eyebrow. "Just because I know you, you think I'm going to give you a free pass?"

"I guess not."

"Right. You have to earn a spot in my bed."

Embarrassment crashed through her. How was she ever going to compete with the other women? With experienced subs? She'd fall short every time.

And did she even want to? Freddie wasn't going to be the safe space she thought he'd be. But was that even what she wanted? It certainly wasn't what she came to the club for. She was seeking someone to push her limits and give her what she needed without asking.

The way her body throbbed for his attention, she suddenly sure it had to be Freddie.

"Like I said, think about all of it, Kylie. If you come here again, our next chat might not be so innocent. I will push your boundaries. Now, get off my lap."

. . .

After what had transpired on Thursday night, Kylie found daily routine tasks much harder to complete. At the gym, she'd messed up paperwork on more than one occasion. She'd nearly rear-ended another car at a light. She'd put orange juice in her coffee instead of creamer. Her brain was a scrambled mess.

All she could think about was Freddie. He occupied her thoughts twenty-four hours a day, it seemed. She couldn't escape him, even in her sleep. She woke in the night with a feverish sweat and an ache between her legs that a vibrator just couldn't cure.

She wanted what he'd promised. Hot sex. She wanted him to test her limits, to push her past her comfort zone. She was aching for his touch and desperate for his kiss. While there had been many attractive Doms at the club and some who had shown interest in her, once she saw Freddie, she knew she needed to have him. She just wasn't sure how to make it happen.

Early on Saturday morning, kneeling on her yoga mat, Kylie was in sunbird pose with her right arm extended forward and her left leg reaching backward when she noticed movement by the door.

Glancing over, she tried not to smile when she spotted Freddie standing with a drink tray containing one cup and a brown paper bag. Only moments before, she'd heard the front door open and close, but she had assumed it was her sister leaving for work.

"Don't mind me," he said, leaning in the doorframe. "Carry on."

She felt his stare travel over her body. In tight black leggings and a matching sports bra, Kylie hadn't expected company during her morning yoga routine. Under his scrutiny, it was impossible to simply continue, knowing he'd be watching each movement she made. She switched to stretch the opposite side before directing her gaze back at him. "You never used to look at me like that."

Though his facial features didn't show it, she saw the hint of a smile in his eyes. "Not that you noticed, no. But I've definitely looked at you, Kylie. A lot."

She blushed. He was much better at playing this game than she was. "What are you doing here? I thought Janet left. I didn't realize you were here."

"She did just leave. She's late for work but was thrilled when she found out I'd brought you both coffee and doughnuts. She kissed me on the cheek and told me how nice I am."

Kylie snorted. She used to think that, too.

"You disagree?" He set the tray down on the bookshelf by the door. "One day, I might show you just how nice I can be."

Any measure of calm she'd discovered that morning fled. Her heartbeat raced, and suddenly, she wanted his hands on her body. Kylie moved briefly into child's pose but then realized she couldn't see him, and she wasn't entirely sure how she felt about that. Quickly, she shifted into cobra so she didn't lose eye contact.

"I was supposed to meet your brother this morning. Drive him to the rink."

He and X had a pickup game of hockey to attend. "He had to go to the hospital. Late call for a patient in labor. He might have to meet you at the rink." X probably hadn't contacted Freddie because it had been three in the morning when he'd gotten the call, and he was likely too busy at work to remember to text his friend.

"Or he might miss it altogether," he supplied. "Janet told me."

"Then why are you still here?"

"Like I said, I brought coffee. I couldn't possibly have stayed for any other reason, right?"

It dawned on her then that they were alone. She was alone in the house with a Dom—a man who had whispered naughty things in her ear just two nights ago.

Heart pounding, palms sweating, Kylie pushed upward into downward facing dog. Deliberately provoking him with her ass up in the air, her body vulnerable to his advances, she closed her eyes. A moment later, he was there.

His big hands encircled her hips and drew her back further against his crotch. An erection strained against the front of his pants.

She walked her hands back a bit to ease the pressure on her muscles and tried to focus on her breathing.

"Did you think about me last night? The night before?"

Kylie was silent. Of course she had. He was all she could think about—every minute of every damned day.

His grip tightened. "I asked you a question."

And if she didn't answer, she wondered what would happen, but she decided to answer honestly. "Yes. I did. I can't stop thinking about it."

"It?"

"You. All the things you said."

"Good." He put a little space between them and ran his fingers down the back of her thighs, then upward again. "You have a terrific ass, Kylie."

She didn't reply.

"Have you ever been fucked here? Has any man ever touched you there?"

She felt her face redden. Luckily, he couldn't see her embarrassment. "I can't believe you just asked me that!"

"I'll take that as a no." Again, his erection returned, rubbing along her butt cheeks. "Your ass makes me think of all sorts of things—how it would feel to take you there. If you'd enjoy it, but right now, I can't help but think about what it would be like to spank it."

She tensed as his hand coasted over her outer thigh. "You have firm muscles, but I'm betting it would still jiggle a little from my palm." That hand moved between her legs, rubbing up and down her inner thigh. "I bet it turns nice and red real quick, too."

She tried not to pant. Hell, in downward dog, with his hands all over her, his dirty words, and his groin pressed against her, she tried not to drool.

"Just like your face. It turns beat red when you get embarrassed."

"Do you often think about smacking me?"

"Spanking, Kylie. Not smacking." His hand returned to her ass, cupping one cheek. "And yes. Very often."

She was sure he was going to spank her right then, but instead, he moved away from her. She looked back at him, accusation in her tone when she demanded, "What are you doing?"

He pressed a finger to his lips, indicating she should be quiet.

"Freddie?" her brother called from the front door.

"In here," he replied.

Kylie's arms gave out, and she collapsed on the floor. Quickly, she scrambled into a cross-legged sitting pose in the middle of her mat and attempted to adjust her hair.

Freddie's eyes shone with glee. "Like I said, a beautiful shade of red."

Her gaze widened, but she couldn't do anything about her face now. It simply grew redder under his stare. Seconds later, Xavier showed up at the entrance to the living room. He clapped Freddie on the back. "Sorry I didn't text you, but I'm glad I caught you in time."

"No worries." Freddie stepped backward, his feet inching further away from her mat. "You about ready to go?"

"Yeah, I've just got to run upstairs for a minute."

"Sounds good. I'll meet you at the door."

X was about to leave, but then he seemed to notice her sitting there. "Hey, sis, did you fall or something? Your face is all red."

Unimpressed, she glanced at Freddie and then back at her brother. "Yep. I fell."

Shaking his head, he exited, leaving her once more alone with Freddie. They both listened as his footsteps mounted the stairs before falling heavily on the carpeted hallway leading to his bedroom.

Freddie closed the gap between them and crouched down next to her. He grasped her chin and directed her gaze to his.

She swallowed and tried not to seem too desperate when she said, "So, you're leaving?"

"Eager, are you?"

Her blush deepened. She hated how badly she wanted him, how she longed for him to pick her for his holiday misdeeds. Trying to downplay her interest, she replied, "Curious."

He scoffed. "Will you be at the club this week?"

She wanted to beg him to kiss her, but instead, she answered him. "I'll be there on Thursday again. Hannah is taking me."

"Your friend with the two Doms? I remember her from last year."

Kylie frowned. She recalled Hannah mentioning how she'd tried to get on his naughty list last year. How close had she come to being his sub instead of Darrell and Derek's? Had Freddie kissed her? Touched her? Jealousy spiked through her, which was stupid. She hadn't even known she wanted him two days ago.

"Kylie." Freddie drew her attention, and as though he'd read every thought she'd just had, he asked, "How do you feel about sharing?"

"What?" Was he talking about Hannah? Or was he talking about Hannah and her Doms? Did he expect her to share him with another sub?

"Is sharing good or bad?" he urged.

She considered his question for a moment. During her year of teaching, she'd repeatedly said the same motto when it came to sharing. The exact words slowly slipped out as she sat under his piercing stare, "Sharing is caring."

A smile crept onto his beautiful face. "Great answer." With his thumb, he rubbed her lower lip. Her lips parted ever so slightly, a gasp escaping them. "Thursday, I want you to wear something easy for you to remove."

Intrigued by the command, she uttered one syllable. "Yes."

"Good. Don't forget." In the distance, they heard her brother's footsteps coming closer once more. Freddie leaned closer. "I'd hate to have to punish you already."

Within seconds, he was gone, out of the room, and waiting at the front door when her brother descended the stairs. X sent her a little wave as he passed by the doorway.

She waved back, but her attention was on the coffee tray on the bookshelf. He'd brought her and Janet coffee and doughnuts. He really was a nice guy, yet at the same time, she was pretty sure he'd be happy to have to dole out punishment to her come Thursday night.

Chapter Four

Kylie's phone vibrated.

Focusing on how Darrell's body moved against hers, she ignored the text message, but a moment later, she caught sight of Freddie. His gaze was dark and brooding and focused entirely on her.

"I'm not sure our resident Santa Claus likes to share," Darrell whispered in her ear.

"That's silly," Kylie told him. He'd talked with her about sharing just that weekend, and he'd been all for it. "He's had women on his lap all night. He's been kissing and touching them."

"Oh, sounds like you might be a little jealous too."

Kylie scoffed. Oh, fine, she was jealous. She hated how women flocked to him. She hated how she'd sought him out immediately when she'd arrived, and then she'd given him a wave only to be dismissed.

So she'd continued on with Hannah and joined her Doms at their booth for a drink and conversation. Hannah had summed up her relationship with Freddie so that Darrell and Derek were up to speed, and soon, she found herself on the dancefloor with them again.

Tonight, she'd worn a high-waisted white skirt that buttoned up the side and a short-sleeved crop top with a deep V that showed off her cleavage. She'd skipped a bra, and the only thing holding her top together was a big brown button. Her boots, the same thigh-highs she'd worn the week before, would be the most challenging part of her outfit to remove. She'd followed his order for clothing she could easily remove, yet he'd still dismissed her.

The tight skirt made it difficult to dance in, especially considering all the grinding Darrell seemed to want to do, but she could make out the shape of his erection each time he brushed against her ass. Knowing he found her attractive made it a little easier to watch Freddie with the endless supply of women competing for his lap.

"Maybe a little jealous," she confessed, as she actively tried to ignore Freddie.

"My money is on you. You're a BDSM virgin, which is appealing in itself. You haven't yet been broken in, plus he's already been crushing on you in the past. He'll pick you."

"And if he doesn't?"

"Based on the daggers he's shooting my way, that won't happen."

When she glanced his way this time, she noticed Freddie had cleared the women away from his booth. He raised his finger and crooked it, summoning her.

She saw red. "I can't believe he just did that."

Darrell laughed. "You'd better get over there."

She recoiled. "Not after that!"

"Let me give you a little advice. Being a naughty sub is one thing, but outright defiance is another. He wants you there. He's obviously not happy that I've been dancing with you. You need to go to him now, or I'll have to change my bet."

Kylie hated being summoned like a dog. "Fine."

"And maybe you two should have a chat about guidelines. If sharing isn't your thing, you need to tell him now."

She sighed. She didn't have any right to be jealous. He hadn't made her any promises. He'd been clear about what he wanted from her. She reminded herself that it was only one night he promised these subs. Only December twenty-third. She knew he'd fly back to the States come the New Year. If anything happened between them, it would be over when he left.

Leaving Darrell and what suddenly felt like comfort and safety behind, she headed toward Freddie.

"What?" she snapped, a little louder than she'd intended.

Freddie raised an eyebrow. Motioning to his lap, he said, "Sit."

Grumbling, she perched herself on his lap.

"Why are you so surly? Did I interrupt your fun?" he mocked.

She crossed her arms under her chest and looked him in the eye. "I don't like being summoned like a dog."

Freddie grasped her chin and pulled her close, so close she felt his breath against her lips. "If I ask you to come to me crawling on your hands and knees across the fucking floor, you will do it. Or you can consider yourself crossed off my naughty list."

It felt so much like a dismissal when he released her chin. Why did it turn her on when he said such awful things to her? Did he do it on purpose?

Kylie wasn't sure whether to retort or not when he continued. "Besides, you didn't answer my text."

The vibration. She shifted and pulled her phone out from where it rested against her breast. He'd written two words. Come here.

Still, it was a summons as far as she was concerned. "Are you jealous, Freddie?"

He ignored her question. "You call me Santa when we're at the club."

She rolled her eyes.

"Do you know how many spankings I give for each roll of the eyes?"

Kylie straightened. Suddenly, playing this game seemed more fun than dancing with Darrell. Darrell was great, but Freddie was exciting. Freddie made her panties wet with little more than a few whispered words. "Two?" she guessed.

"Five. The first time." His hand touched her bare thigh. "If she does it again, she gets another twelve."

"And after the third time."

Freddie's gaze was unwavering. "There is no third time."

She wasn't sure if that meant he abandoned her as a sub if she did it three times or if two punishments were all it took to get his subs in line.

His hand curved around her thigh. "I can't wait to spank your ass, Kylie."

"What makes you think I'll misbehave? Maybe I'll be the perfect sub."

"I can't even count on one hand all the things you've done wrong tonight. My hand will be on your bare ass for sure."

Her nipples tightened at the thought.

"But that will have to wait for another night." His lips grazed her ear. "I asked you about sharing."

"Yes." Nervously, Kylie glanced toward Hannah and her Doms, then toward some of the women who flocked to Freddie. She wasn't entirely sure she was okay with sharing him. "What did you mean by that?"

"I certainly didn't mean for you to let your friend's Dom have free reign of your body."

"I didn't!"

"Don't argue." He laid a finger over her lips. "From now on, you will only allow touches from those who have my permission."

"*What?*" Kylie jumped. How was that fair? She might be a novice, but she knew he shouldn't be asking her such things without some kind of commitment. "You can't dictate that. You're not my Dom. Besides, are you going to stop touching all those other women?"

He sighed. She'd displeased him, that much was obvious, but right now, she was too outraged to care. "If you want on my naughty list, you need to show me you can handle my instructions. Without questioning me."

"This sounds like your way of keeping me to yourself while still getting to do whatever you please."

"That's not true. I simply require that you only be touched by those I've approved and given permission to. I want you to have pleasure, and that pleasure doesn't necessarily have to come from me."

"Prove it."

"I was hoping you'd say that." His smile was wicked.

She realized she'd made a mistake. He'd baited her. What made her think she could play this game as well as him?

"Look up. Do you see that man coming toward us?"

Kylie glanced up and noticed the crowd parting around one man. He was as tall as Freddie but with wider shoulders and broader hips. His hairy chest was bare, and tight black leather encased his legs. He was all muscle and intimidation.

She gulped. What had she gotten herself into?

"His name is Conan."

"Like the barbarian?" she rasped.

Freddie leaned toward her, his body rubbing against her back. "Exactly like. And don't pretend the idea doesn't fascinate you. I saw how your body moved forward."

She tried to sit back, to deny it, but he pressed against her, keeping her pinned in place.

"I bet your nipples are tight, and your pussy is wet just at the thought of me letting Conan have you tonight."

Inhaling, she didn't dare tell him that his words, more so than the approaching man, aroused her.

"Will you show me how much you're willing to obey? How far you're willing to go to get on my list? To get into my bed?"

Unable to help herself, she rubbed against his leg. She needed him badly. "Yes."

"Then tonight, you belong to Conan. He has my permission to touch you. No other Dom but him and I. Do you understand?"

"I think so. Where will the three of us go?"

Freddie's chuckle tickled the hairs on her nape. "No, no. I'm going to watch. From here." As Conan drew closer, Freddie pointed to the open stage. "We're all going to watch."

"No." She gasped.

"Yes, Kylie. You've seen what happens at this club. No one will bat an eye at what happens to you up there. And your privacy is protected here, I promise."

"Freddie, I can't do that."

"Santa," he corrected. "And yes, you can. Know that it pleases me to watch. Know that I'm down here pretending it's me doing everything to you. Know that when I get home tonight, I'm going to jerk off thinking about all the dirty things he's about to do to you."

Kylie wanted to know why he didn't just do them himself, but she supposed it was kind of hot being put on display for him. But she doubted she could go through with being put on display.

"I want you to show everyone in this room how badly you want me. Just how much you're willing to take in order to have my cock deep inside you."

Her vaginal walls contracted. How was he making it all sound so sexy, so appealing? God only knew what was about to happen to her on that stage, and yet here she was imagining Freddie with his hand wrapped around his dick, beating off to thoughts of her.

Was she really going to do this?

She didn't have time to decide.

Suddenly, Conan was in front of her, towering over them.

"So this is her, huh?" He grunted.

As his gaze roamed over her, Kylie wasn't sure whether she should be amused, scared, or turned on.

"This is her." Behind her, Freddie stroked a hand down her back. "Kylie."

Conan leaned closer to examine her. "No, I don't think I'm going to call you that. You're Santa's little slut, aren't you?"

Wide-eyed, Kylie wasn't sure how to reply or if she was even supposed to.

He seemed to enjoy her indecision. "Well, tonight, you're going to be my little slut."

She scooted back on Freddie's lap, making the behemoth laugh. Freddie whispered to her, "You have nothing to be afraid of, Kylie. Conan is a friend and a business acquaintance. I wouldn't let anyone touch you if I didn't trust them. Know that for everything he does, he has my permission, and ultimately, it will please you."

"Are you sure?"

"Yes, Kylie. Your safe word is mistletoe, do you understand me?"

She nodded.

"Say it."

Staring up at the ape, she replied, "Mistletoe."

"Good girl." Freddie placed a kiss on the side of her neck. "You won't need it tonight, though. And if you do, you'll never make it through what else I have planned for you."

This time, she swung her gaze back to his. He was giving her to someone else, which wasn't the naughtiest thing he planned to do with her.

"You about done, Santa?" Conan asked with an exaggerated sigh.

"She's all yours."

She'd been staring at Freddie when those final words hit her. She whipped her head back around. "Wait. No."

"Great." Conan rubbed his enormous hands together, and for a moment, Kylie thought about her safe word, but before she could decide, Conan reached down, seized her by the waist, and hoisted her over his shoulder.

Chapter Five

His shoulder was like granite beneath her. With each hard step he took, she tried not to grasp at his back for extra support, terrified that he'd drop her. In the distance, she caught sight of Hannah, Derek, and Darrell. The Doms were smirking. Hannah was giving her a thumbs up.

Oh my God. They were going to watch her fall apart at the hands of this big brute of a man. And she knew then that she would fall apart. She would submit to him because it would bring her one step closer to Freddie.

Conan mounted the stairs to the stage and set her on her feet, but one of his hands shackled hers, keeping her from running, not that she'd get very far in her heels. From the wing, a woman rolled out a small trolley and bowed her head to Conan. When he nodded, she turned and vacated the stage, leaving Kylie alone with Conan before a room full of people.

One glance out at the club eased her mind. Most people continued with their dancing and playing, but very few paid attention to the stage.

Kylie peered around Conan to peek at the cart. The only thing on it was ribbon. Lots and lots of red ribbon, multiple rolls, in fact. "What are you going to—"

He flashed her a warning look. "You don't get to speak unless spoken to."

"I'm new at this, cut me some—"

Again, he didn't let her finish. This time, he tugged her close, nearly knocking her off balance. One hand roughly clasped hers, and the other grabbed her hair and yanked hard. With her face tilted up rather awkwardly, she was forced to look him in the eye.

"Unless you're uttering your safe word or I've asked you a question, you don't get to speak." He yanked once more on her hair. She grimaced but didn't make a sound. "Understood?"

Unsure if she should reply or not, she merely nodded. That couldn't get her in trouble.

"Good."

She staggered a bit when he released her.

"Now undress."

"What?" Shocked, the word slipped out. Instantly, she covered her mouth with both hands.

Conan's eyes narrowed, and in one step, he closed the gap that had formed between them. "Is it that you don't listen, or that you don't understand? Or are you just a little brat who needs to be punished?"

This time, she defended herself. "It was an accident."

"There are no accidents." Grabbing her, he spun her to face the crowd. "I knew that you'd stall and find a way to take your time with my instruction, but now I'm taking that away from you." His giant hands fell on the button holding her top together. "Now, everyone will watch your shame as I strip you bare for their eyes."

Why did that make her knees weak? She couldn't say, but she didn't have time to dwell on it. As Conan had promised, he made quick work of removing her clothing. The button gave way easily with one little tug. In a swift move, he worked the piece off her shoulders and tossed it to the far side of the stage, leaving her breasts bare and exposed.

Freddie was watching.

Kylie swallowed. She tried to find him in the crowd, but her gaze was shaky.

This was the first time he'd see her naked. Would he be pleased?

"No bra. Nice," Conan said from behind her. His large hands came up and encircled her breasts, lifting their weight in his palms. He fondled her for a moment, just kneading her flesh before scissoring her nipples between his fingers, pulling them forward so much so that she had to take a step forward to keep from falling. "Very nice tits, slut. He'll be pleased when he gets to touch them. As pleased as I am."

For a second, he rubbed against her backside, showing her just how much he enjoyed touching her. His erection was massive against her lower back. The man was built proportionately.

His nose trailed down her neck. She could hear him inhale. "Santa has given me permission to touch but not to taste." He kept her nipples pinched between his fingers. "Which is a shame because I bet you taste as sweet as candy."

Again, she nearly lost her balance. He was talking about her pussy—about eating her out. Why couldn't he have strapped her to something, a St. Andrew's cross or a bench of some sort? Something to support her when she couldn't do so herself.

"But he's requested something else entirely." His hands skimmed down her sides, and he began working on the buttons of her skirt. There were only four. Soon, she'd be left in nothing but her panties and boots, and she doubted he'd let her keep either for long. "Do you know what Shibari is?"

A frown pinched her brow as she thought. "Is that the rope stuff?"

"Rope stuff." He chuckled. The final button came free. Her skirt landed next to her top. Her panties covered very little in the front, just a small triangle of material, but the back covered even less. Thong panties.

She closed her eyes as his hand traced the strap from the front, around her hip, and down between her ass cheeks.

"Fuck, that's nice."

He pulled the strap enough to wedge the front against her lips, making her gasp. He pulled a little tighter. Without meaning to, she went on tiptoe.

His voice returned to her ear. "Shibari is the Japanese style of bondage. It's what I do, what I've studied."

"Studied?" Again, she forgot she wasn't supposed to speak.

"I'll let that one go," he told her, though he really didn't, considering he pulled her panties even tighter, pressing them flush against her pussy lips and down enough that a bit of her pubic hair peeked out the top. "Yes, studied. If you don't take precautions, take the time to learn, then binding someone can be very dangerous."

He jerked the panties down her thighs and urged her legs apart enough that they would still drop, unhindered to the stage floor.

Boots. She stood before a crowd of strangers in nothing but a pair of thigh-high boots.

"Now, follow my next set of instructions to the letter, or I promise you I'll spank you in front of all these people."

Kylie glanced over her shoulder. What would he have her do now?

"I want you to bend at the waist; do not crouch. Bend, undo, and remove your boots."

She took a moment to consider that task. She'd be exposed to him—her ass and pussy on display for his gaze. She supposed she should be thankful he hadn't asked her to turn around first. Knowing her first spanking shouldn't be public and shouldn't be from Conan, Kylie didn't argue.

Bending at the waist, she removed the boots and tossed them, one at a time, to the side of the stage where the rest of her clothing lay.

"The panties, too," he told her.

Without hesitation, they joined the pile.

"Good girl," he praised her. "You're learning. Keep this up, and I might even let you come."

Her gaze darted to him. Was that something that could happen? Was that something Freddie would allow? And even if it was, would she be able to? It was rare she was ever able to climax with a man. Generally, she had to do it on her own.

He reached for the first roll of ribbon. He unwound a considerable length of it until the spool it came on was empty. "Normally, I use rope, but tonight, I'm going to wrap you like a Christmas present before I deliver you back to Santa."

He placed the wide ribbon over her breasts, covering her peaked nipples, and pulled it tight. She felt him cross the ribbon against her back before bringing an end up under both arms and down over her shoulders. It didn't take him long before he completed her bustier and tied the ends at her back, where she was sure he'd created a big bow to hold it all together.

Glancing down, she realized he'd fashioned a top—a very skimpy one—from the ribbon. One length of it went below her bosom and a second strip across her nipples, leaving the fullness of her breasts exposed and pushing against the ribbon. Two shoulder straps completed the look.

He circled around in front of her, straightening pieces here and there until it was perfect. When he'd finished, he traced along the satin, his finger slipping beneath to graze her nipple.

She gasped.

His gaze rose from what he'd been doing to look into her eyes. A smile played across his lips. He knew the effect he was having on her.

Returning to the cart, he told her, "Now for panties."

She grew a little weak in the knees, thinking of satin rubbing against her most intimate places.

He unrolled another length of ribbon, but he left it on the tray. Stepping up behind her, he grasped her hips. "You're going to need to spread your legs a bit."

Gulping, she stepped her feet apart, giving him the required space.

"Good girl." His palms coasted down her bare hips toward the apex of her thighs. "You're definitely learning. But I'm wondering just how much you're enjoying this." With that as her only warning, he cupped her mound.

Unconsciously, she stepped her feet further apart. He chuckled but took the hint. One long finger coasted downward, rubbing over her clit before dipping just slightly into her entrance. It had been so long since anyone had touched her.

Conan took a bit of her wetness and spread it over her lips before returning to her hole once more, this time plunging two thick fingers inside. It was almost too much. She moved to grab his hand to stop him from pushing further in, but he was faster. Stopping her hand, he murmured against the skin of her neck. "You are enjoying this." He didn't push in any deeper but eased out and slowly back in. "Tell me, is it the crowd watching, the stranger touching you, or knowing that the man you want most has ordered this? Has ordered me to touch you? To strip you?"

"All of it," she answered honestly. It was all so new, fresh, and much more than she could have imagined. His words had brought forth another wave of wetness between her thighs. He was quick to slather her clit in her juices and continue to pump her with his hand.

"Of course you do because you're a filthy little slut who wants to get fucked."

She gasped and bucked as he brought her closer to orgasm.

"But he's going to make you wait, you know that, right? He'll make you wait until the end of the month, and even then, he might pick someone else to keep his bed warm. What do you think of that?"

Kylie frowned and shook her head. She had to believe he wouldn't put her through all of this for nothing. She searched for him in the crowd but still couldn't place him. It was too dark. There were too many people. Was he watching? Was he observing his friend finger fuck her?

"If that happens, if he doesn't pick you"—his thumb pressed against her clitoris as he rubbed two fingers high inside her, pushing her closer to release—"you can come to me. If you ask me really nicely, all pretty and sweet and begging for my cock instead, I might just give it to you."

Kylie groaned and trembled. She was so close.

But Conan pulled away.

She suddenly felt cold with him no longer standing next to her. She hung her head backward and groaned when he came at her with the ribbon once more. She'd been so damn close.

Without saying a word, she let Conan know her fury with her icy glare. He laughed. Stretching out the ribbon, he told her, "Not to worry, little one, I'll get you there again, but whether or not I let you come depends on you."

He set about creating a set of bottoms very much the same way he had made her top. Soon, she was covered, somewhat decently, with straps around her hips and tied at the back. This time, he'd created two bows rather than one. The satin pieces that stretched and rubbed against her pussy lips felt so good she struggled not to reach down and press them harder against her. She was still wet from the almost climax he'd denied her, so she knew it wouldn't take much to get off.

But before she brought the idea to fruition, he grabbed more ribbon and urged her to bring her arms in front of her—her wrists and palms against one another. Three times, he bound her wrists and arms with the ribbon. Three bows decorated her arms, holding her close together. She tested them, pulling slightly at first, then harder. They weren't just snug—they were secure. He certainly knew what he was doing. Kylie was unsure if she'd need scissors to get out of the knots he'd created.

He examined his work, dipping his finger into her cleavage.

"Perfect." He straightened a few more pieces of ribbon, adjusted one bow, and stepped back to allow the crowd to see his work.

Kylie glanced down at herself and couldn't help but feel sexy in the specially-created outfit.

"The great thing about these red panties"—he moved next to her—"is this nice little slit right here." He reached between her legs and parted the ribbon so his fingers had access once more for him. "Though, I prefer this little slit." This time he rubbed her pussy lips.

"God," she whispered, her eyes closing. She wished she had a chair, bed, or anything to support her. Instead of offering himself as support, Conan let her stand freely as his fingers worked over her.

"You've been a good girl," he told her with his lips pressed against her hair. "Santa thought you'd give me a hard time, but no. Which makes me wonder what you'll be like for him. Will you be good for him too?"

She sucked in a breath as he pushed three big fingers inside her. "Yes," she promised.

He chuckled. "I doubt that."

Kylie frowned and tried to focus on what he was doing to her. She had been good. She hadn't fought too much about being on stage. She'd followed his direction unless she slipped up, but nothing she'd done wrong had been on purpose. She'd earned that orgasm as far as she was concerned, and he better fucking deliver.

His fingers stroked in and out of her body. His thumb worked over her clit.

She got closer and closer to that deep, dark edge. Her body began to shake.

Half hoping she'd never be up on this stage again, Kylie took a moment to revel in the exhibitionism. She met the gaze of a few people near the stage, their gazes looking up at her, watching this big man dominating and manipulating her to his will. Then she searched him out once more.

This time, she found him in the crowd. He sat alone in his booth, leaning forward, his stare direct and entirely focused on her.

This is for you, she thought, as Conan thrust into her repeatedly. *All for you.*

"You're so close." Conan's tone was as rough as his fingers. "You have three seconds to beg me for your release, or I will stop."

"What?" Shocked, Kylie shuddered. He couldn't stop now. "No."

"Then beg."

For all of a second, she bit her lip and whimpered. "Please, please let me come." Her legs were shaking, her body so close to bliss.

"Louder." He grabbed a fist full of her hair and pulled her face upward to center her gaze on him. "So he can hear you."

There was no hesitation. She raised her voice, "Please, Conan, please, let me come."

She wasn't sure if Freddie could hear her, but she was sure the sentiment carried across the room. Conan was ruthless as he fingered her, deep and hard and fast. When he told her to come, she let go immediately, tears dripping down her cheeks, her legs wobbling beneath her. She cried out.

When she'd finished, Conan released her hair and stepped away from her. She collapsed to the floor, her tied wrists supporting her as she sat on her knees, her head bent and her body shaking.

She couldn't believe what had just happened. She let someone —a stranger, no less—finger her in front of a room of people, and worse still, she'd begged him to do it.

What was happening to her? And why could all she think about was begging Freddie to do the same thing to her?

Five minutes later, Conan had carried her off to one of the private rooms. The girl who had dragged out the trolley followed behind them with Kylie's boots and clothing in her hands. Was this girl Conan's sub? And why had he taken her somewhere private? Freddie hadn't mentioned anything about this.

"Why did we come here?" Kylie glanced around the room. A bed, a St. Andrew's cross, and a spanking bench were the only furniture in the room. Off to one side was a door. She assumed it was a washroom.

Conan didn't bother to answer her. Instead, he directed the other woman. "Put her things on the bed."

With only a nod, the woman complied. She dropped the items on the red bedspread and retreated from the room, leaving the door open.

"Stand here." Conan put her down before straightening her ribbons. He pulled yet another strand of ribbon from his pocket, fashioned it into a bow, and tied it in her hair. "Don't move." Footsteps approached the door. Conan turned in their direction before heading toward them. He glanced back at her, "Remember what I said about the end of the month. I'll be here."

When he walked out of the room, leaving her alone, she quickly raised her bound hands and wiped at her cheeks. What was she supposed to do now? Get dressed?

Kylie examined the bows. She doubted she'd be able to get herself free. Would she need to return to the club and ask for help?

Just then, she heard their voices at the door. Conan and Freddie's.

Relief rushed through her until she listened to their conversation.

"You said I wouldn't be able to get her to beg," Conan told Freddie.

"An oversight on my part. I didn't think she would. Not publicly." His voice dropped a bit. "Not privately either."

Kylie's eyes widened. Uh-oh. Had she made a mistake?

"I think I deserve a prize for that."

Freddie's laugh was harsh. "I don't think so."

"She does have the prettiest little mouth."

"Get your own sub to suck your cock then, stop daydreaming about mine."

Kylie's mouth fell open. *Oh my God. Were they really discussing a blowjob?* Then, a second thought. *Did he just call me his?*

Conan laughed. "Maybe one day we can trade."

Freddie didn't reply, leaving Kylie to wonder exactly what that meant. She didn't want to watch another woman go down on him, and for that matter, he was the only one she wanted to taste, to enjoy. Her antics on the stage had been at his command, not something she wanted to become routine.

"Enjoy her, my friend." There was a sound like Conan was slapping Freddie on the back before footsteps started away from the door.

"Fantastic work with the ribbon."

Conan's laugh was all that followed.

Freddie stepped into the room and closed the door. Leaning against it, he stood watching her. His gaze went from her head down to her feet and back up, stopping on her thighs, hips, stomach, and breasts. He ended with a quick nod to the bow in her hair.

"Well, aren't you just the loveliest Christmas present?"

Heat rushed to her face, and she took a step toward him. "Freddie, I—"

"No." His tone was sharp. "You don't get to speak."

She snapped her jaw shut. This no-talking thing was a real bitch. Thinking about what Conan had said, about her not challenging him but how she'd challenge Freddie, had her smiling. "But Freddie—"

"One thing." As he approached, his eyes flashed with some emotion, anger, excitement, she wasn't sure. "There's only one thing I want your mouth to be doing right now."

After the talk of blowjobs, she half expected him to begin undoing his pants as he came toward her, but instead, his arms came around her. One hand tangled in her hair, and the other grabbed her waist. He crashed into her, his lips slamming onto hers in an all-consuming kiss that obliterated her childhood illusions of him.

He didn't kiss like a Disney prince. There was no lingering eye contact, no slight tilting of the head. No, he was greedy and took her breath from her in a dirty, filthy mouth fuck of a kiss, his tongue invading her mouth and leaving her dizzy.

She would have clutched at his shoulders, but with her hands tied and trapped between their bodies, she could do nothing but pray he held her up.

Luckily, just as her knees felt as though they would no longer hold her up, he backed her toward the wall, his mouth never leaving hers. She felt him nudge her legs apart to thrust his thigh between hers. Immediately, she began grinding against it. She couldn't seem to help herself.

When he let her up for air, she gasped in a few breaths, then told him, "Untie my hands." She wanted to touch him. His naked chest was hot where it crushed against her, but she wanted to touch more of him, particularly the large cock pressing into her midsection.

"No." One hand was buried in her hair and held her in place as his mouth ravished hers once more.

She groaned and bucked, trying to get even closer to him. She felt hot, as though her body was on fire, aching for more of him.

"I want to touch you," she pleaded the next time they broke apart. "I need you inside me."

His grip grew tighter, pulling almost painfully at her hair. "I said no."

The firm tone, the rigid grip, and the hard thigh between her legs were enough to make her combust. "Freddie, please."

Scorching a path down her neck, his lips set her pulse tripping. "That word is awfully pretty coming from your mouth. Even prettier when it's directed at me."

"If you can't tell that I want you..." She trailed off when he dragged the ribbon covering her breasts down and sucked her nipple into his mouth. "Ahh, Freddie."

He gave it the same attention he'd given her mouth: hot, feverish, and urgent. Briefly stopping, he pushed her hands lower and ground his pelvis against them before switching to suckle at her other breast. It was difficult, but she managed to shift her hands, so with each thrust, his dick rubbed along her palms.

"I have to make you come. I have to see you fall apart again." His breath was hot against her skin.

As much as Kylie wanted to deny that two orgasms in one night would be impossible for her, she already knew it would be a lie. She was still wet from her recent climax, and now, with Freddie so close, with his aftershave filling her nostrils, his lips on her body, and his thigh relieving the building pressure between her legs, she knew it was possible. Only with Freddie. Only because of him.

She rubbed herself against him, growing more frantic for the release he offered her.

He straightened and pinned her once more, this time with a hand on her throat rather than tangled in her hair. His gaze was so intense she tried to look away, but he controlled her movements.

"Once you've come, once you've left a hot, wet spot right there on my pants, I'm going to come all over your tits."

The noise she made was feral—half-human, half-wild beast—as she tried to get away from him. It was too much, too many sensations. But he wouldn't let her, wouldn't even let her look away. She didn't know what she wanted.

"That's right, baby, show me how badly you want it. Show me how badly you want to fuck me."

She screamed. She couldn't help it. In that moment, she worked her hips, pounding against his hard thigh, gliding her hands against his rock-hard erection. In seconds, she was coming. Wave after wave swept through her body as the most intense climax she'd ever had racked her body.

Freddie's mouth descended on hers, gathering her groans and guttural sounds.

Before she had a chance to fully recover, he shoved her to her knees, dragged his Santa pants down just enough to release his cock. With a couple of strokes, he was coming, spilling his hot, white seed onto her breasts.

Once again, tears streaked down her face as she tried to catch her breath. What was happening to her? She'd never come like that before. She'd always needed penetration of some kind, and never had she experienced something so powerful.

"Fuck, you're so goddamn beautiful like that." He swirled a finger in the liquid on her chest, rubbing it across her cleavage and down to her nipple. "Covered in my cum."

Even though she was still wrecked from her orgasm, his words had her on edge again. Did she really have to wait until December twenty-third to get more than just a taste of him?

He instructed her to stay while he disappeared into the adjoining room. He returned with tissues. Kneeling on the floor, she looked up at him as he tenderly wiped her clean.

For the first time, she realized how important Freddie was becoming to her. How much she needed what he had to offer her. She'd always known there was a chance he wouldn't pick her for his misdeeds this holiday season, but now she entertained an even worse fear. What would happen if he did pick her? How would she be able to walk away from him after the holidays?

Chapter Six

Anytime she wasn't with a client, Kylie was daydreaming about the events of last Thursday night. She'd tried to keep herself busy, filling out paperwork and spreadsheets, offering to help restock cupboards, and getting on the treadmill, all to try and dispense some of this extra pent-up sexual frustration she was experiencing.

Earlier in the day, she'd received a vague text message from Freddie:

> I'm sending a package to you at work rather than at home. I didn't want Janet to snoop.

Excited to see what it was, she wanted next Thursday night to come faster. She had no idea what Freddie had planned for this coming week, but she knew she was eager to participate.

At the beginning of the week, she'd gone shopping with Janet, which had helped occupy her mind a bit more than the busy work she was trying to focus on. Each year, they threw a pre-Christmas party a week or so before the holidays hit. It was a tradition Janet had started a few years back when she'd first been hired at the fashion magazine as a photographer. Kylie and X teased her each time the party drew nearer because it was just an excuse for her to see her boss outside of work. She had a terrible crush on the owner of the magazine. Each year, if he came, he stayed for maybe half an hour and barely gave Janet any of his time. Kylie was sure he was there to hit on the models Janet invited.

The models were why so many of X's friends also showed up. As she'd perused through the aisles of the liquor store, stocking up for the party, she'd thought back to the previous years and tried to recall if Freddie had hit on any of the models. She wished she'd paid more attention. Was he into that skinny, barely-fed look? She knew he'd been photographed with models before at charity events, but she didn't think he'd dated any of them. Not seriously, anyway.

Was he more into her body type? She was fit, which was mostly a side effect of her job, but she had a little bulk on her. Her shoulders were broader than she liked. She was happy with her boobs, a good C-cup, and her ass was firm and just the right handful for a man, she thought. Her legs weren't as long as she'd like, but she figured her other assets made up for it.

When she and her sister had been in the grocery store, collecting all the non-perishable items they'd need for the party: chips and dip, pop, red Solo cups, and more, Kylie had asked her a serious question, "Why do you still even bother with your boss when that guy, what's his name, Emmett, seems to have a thing for you?"

Emmett was one of the models Janet frequently shot for the magazine. He'd come to every party they'd hosted, often followed Janet around, and once, he'd even stayed to help clean up.

Janet had frowned at her. "Emmett just wants to get laid. I haven't been his typical easy conquest, so he keeps trying. But trust me, he's not interested in me. He takes off with any of the models the first chance he gets."

Kylie wasn't sure if Janet was reading the situation right and wondered how to get her to open her eyes, but without spilling the beans about Freddie, she wasn't sure how to convince her that Emmett might be worth a second look.

It wasn't until they got home that Kylie realized Janet had

distracted her with a question about pickles and olives rather than discussing her boss.

Kylie finished registering a new client for the gym and then settled back in her seat. What would the party be like this year? Would things be different with Freddie? How could they not?

"Someone got a delivery!" Hannah announced as she came trotting around the corner with a big red box tied tightly with a white bow. "The card says, 'To Kylie, Ho Ho Ho'. I wonder who it could be from?"

Kylie laughed at Hannah's mischief and glanced around. With no one nearby, she took the box and began pulling at the ribbon. "He texted me to say something was coming today. He didn't want Janet to see it, so he sent it here."

"Ooh, so it's going to be naughty." Hannah rubbed her hands together and peered at the box.

Inside was a slutty green elf costume. It was a short little dress that would barely cover her ass cheeks, and if she wasn't careful, it would reveal her gender to anyone who took a close look. She didn't miss the fact that he hadn't sent underwear with it. Did he really expect her to go without?

A thick black belt adorned the middle for decoration, not function, and the bodice was lined with fluffy white trim. The skirt was cut into multiple points, similar to something she'd seen on the Flintstones as a child, but each tip had a little bell on the end.

Accompanying the dress, if she could even call something so short a dress, was a matching green elf hat, a pair of striped knee-high stockings, and black high-heeled stilettos.

Inside the box was a note:

Wear this on Thursday night.

At the bottom was a smaller box with chocolates from her favorite shop. "See, this is what I mean," Kylie said, holding up the box of chocolates. "He sends me this, too. I'm having a lot of trouble equating the nice guy I've known forever, who buys me the chocolates I like, with this Dom that gets me so hot I could die."

Hannah helped herself to a chocolate from the box. "He sent you chocolates and lingerie. Seriously, Kylie, what more could you want?"

"It might be nice to know what's going through his head. Where this is all headed?"

Hannah snorted before putting on the elf hat. She gave her a wicked grin. "Just thank your lucky stars and hold on for the ride."

The second she passed him in the club on Thursday night, he beckoned her to his booth. She attempted, in vain it seemed, not to glare with jealous disdain at the redhead on his lap. The woman was absolutely gorgeous, with a flaming mane of hair and one of the prettiest bodies she'd ever seen outside of a magazine. Her bright cherry lips curved up in a smile that seemed to mock Kylie with each step she took.

Freddie removed his hand from her hip. "Give us a minute, Angel."

The woman, Angel, dipped her gaze down Kylie's body before slipping off his lap. "Of course, Santa." The hint of laughter in her eyes made Kylie more uncomfortable than she already felt. Leaving the house with the longest coat she could find hadn't helped her feel any more relaxed in her outfit. But now her jacket was on a hanger in a room by the door, and no longer able to shield her. She couldn't decide if she looked hot or silly in the outfit he'd picked.

"Sit."

Kylie glared and gnashed her teeth but followed through with the order.

She wasn't sure what issue to address first: her ridiculous outfit or her concern about sharing. They hadn't settled on what exactly sharing meant and how far he planned to take it. But she knew it would be an issue for her, even though she had no right to demand he stop all involvement with the other women on his list.

Before she could speak, he used a finger to ring one of the little bells attached to her dress. "How many times did you think about putting panties on under this?"

She wanted to growl. How had he known her thought process? Five times, she'd dragged various panties up her legs, and each time, she had to take them off. None of them looked right with the outfit, and she knew he'd be pissed if she showed up with underwear on. His choice not to include them in the package had been deliberate.

"I didn't have anything that looked right with it."

"Good, because you're supposed to be naked under here. I want easy access to your pussy tonight."

She squirmed on his lap, eager to discover what would happen as the night progressed.

"I don't want your friend's Doms to touch you tonight. Tonight, you belong to me." He pressed against the edge of the dress, rubbing the green fabric against her mound, dragging one little bell between her legs, the cool metal scraping along her skin. "*This* belongs to me."

"Are you taking me home with you?" Kylie was too hopeful.

He laughed. "No. I'm not breaking my rules for you. But if you behave, you might make it one step closer."

This time, she did growl.

"You're so keen on getting to the finishing line, Kylie. More so than I ever would have thought. When was the last time you've been fucked properly? By someone who knew what they were doing and how to make you come so hard you see stars?"

She couldn't answer that.

"Is it so long you can't remember, or is it because it's never happened?"

"Until this month..." she trailed off, unwilling to admit how he'd affected her.

"Tell me, Kylie."

She glanced up at the ceiling before closing her eyes and confessing. "Battery-operated friends are the only things that come close. Until this month." She opened her eyes to look directly at him. "Until you."

"So you'd do pretty much anything to secure that spot in my bed?"

After feeling his mouth on hers last week, after seeing the look on his face as he spilled his seed all over her, she knew she'd do whatever he asked for a chance at more.

Yet still, she blushed. "Yes," she confessed. When had she become this greedy for sexual satisfaction? "I thought I proved that last week."

"Last week was the tip of the iceberg, babe." He clamped his hand down hard on her thigh, holding her in place. "The woman that was here before you arrived, her name is Angel, and she's about to join us again."

Uh-oh. She didn't like where this was going. What was he going to have her do? She tried to shuffle away from his lap, but his grip grew tighter.

"Angel went home with me last year."

Kylie glanced over to where the woman stood, a few tables away, watching them.

"She's angling for another round...says she'll do anything."

Giving him a stern frown, she tried to decipher if he was lying to get a rise from her or if he was just being boastful. "So you're saying she's my competition."

"The past two times you've been to the club, you've seen the lines for my lap. She's not the only one." His hand rubbed against her bare thigh. "You're not the only one willing to beg me to let you come."

She gritted her teeth. She wanted to deny it, but there'd be no use. Last week, she'd done just that.

"Despite what Angel thinks is going to happen, I don't do repeats."

That brought up a whole lot more questions, but they all died on her tongue when Freddie crooked his finger, indicating that the redhead should join them again.

"What are you doing?"

He shifted them closer to the edge of the booth's bench. "How naughty are you willing to be, Kylie?"

When he pulled her thighs apart, dangling her legs on either side of his and exposing her sex for anyone close enough to see, certainly close enough for Angel to see, Kylie tried to escape. "Seriously, Fred—"

She didn't even get his full name out before his palm slapped over her mouth. "You need to start obeying the rules. You know better than to call me by my name in this club. You call me Santa. And I warned you about questioning me." His lips brushed her ear as his voice dropped to a whisper. "Do it again, and next time you'll find yourself gagged and bound with a bright red ass. Now I don't want to hear another word from your lips unless I ask you a question, and from now on, you do everything I fucking tell you to."

She should have bit his hand, but the way the redhead stood over her, practically laughing while she got scolded, pissed her off too much to fight him. She wasn't sure she wanted any part of whatever Freddie had planned, but her jealousy over this Angel chick was enough to keep her moving forward. No way would she back down and let her take her place.

After a conversation she'd had with Hannah on Friday morning, she was pretty sure Darrell had been right. She was the front-runner. She could give Freddie something he'd wanted for a long time—*her*. When Hannah called her early Friday and demanded that she spill all the details, she didn't hesitate. Hannah claimed it was a first for Freddie to give any sub an O in a private room at the club, and he'd certainly never let his control slip the way he had with her.

He came on her. That had to mean something, right?

"Understood?" His hand lifted from her mouth.

Kylie glanced up into the mocking gaze of the stunning redhead before uttering for the first time, "Yes, Santa."

With his head tilted up to look at Angel, Freddie snapped his fingers and pointed toward the ground. Angel's gaze bounced between him and Kylie.

"You promise?" she asked, cocking her head to the side.

"Have I ever not kept a promise I made to you?" His words

were heavy, and Kylie wondered what sorts of things he'd done to her last year. Had he made her jump through hoops too?

With a saucy little grin, Angel licked her lips and knelt between Kylie's thighs. Kylie's eyes went wide as she tried to close her legs, but Freddie kept her splayed.

The pressure he applied with his fingers held her still, but he instructed, "Unless you're bucking into her face while she fucks you with her tongue, I don't want you to move. Nod if you understand."

Nodding, Kylie tried to stop squirming, but the second Angel's mouth touched her, she jerked. Angel's hands were cold as they coasted along Kylie's inner thighs. Her fingertips grazed over Kylie's entrance as her lips clamped around her clit.

Unsure what to do with her hands, Kylie clenched them into fists, fighting the urge to move or shift or anything. She bit her lip as Angel prodded her with one long, slender finger.

"Put your arms around my neck," Freddie told her.

Raising them, she locked her hands behind his head as instructed.

"Perfect, you're fucking perfect." His palms came up and cupped her breasts through the green material. She arched into his touch, into Angel's mouth. She couldn't help it; it all felt so damn good.

When she realized others were watching the good show they'd put on, Kylie closed her eyes and tried to ignore everyone else. She fixated on the sensations her body was reveling in, focused on the way Angel's tongue twirled around and latched onto her clitoris, on the way her fingers jabbed in and out of her hole, on the way Freddie's fingers pulled at her nipples.

She arched, she bucked, and soon she was begging, pleading with them to let her come. Angel never said a word but continued with her labors.

The bells on her dress jingled with each movement she made.

It was all too much.

With her legs hooked over Freddie's thighs, her body stretched out, she finally fell victim to their efforts and came hard with an unbridled scream.

As her body came back under her control, Angel sat back on her heels, triumph in her eyes.

"Come here," Freddie ordered.

Angel started to rise. The second she was within reach, Freddie grabbed her nape and pulled her in, claiming her in a deep, passionate kiss.

Pain seared through Kylie as she watched the one man she'd ever been desperate for lock lips with another woman, at least until she realized precisely what he was doing. He wasn't just kissing Angel. No, he was tasting her on the other woman's lips, on her tongue.

How did he do it? How did he turn her jealousy into something hot?

"Go get a drink. Put it on my tab. Return when you're done."

Angel nodded and disappeared into the crowd, heading toward the bar.

Kylie tried to straighten her dress in an attempt to cover herself, but Freddie stopped her. "You're proving to be a decent pupil."

Glaring, she shifted to look at him. Decent? She'd just let a woman lick her pussy, and last week she'd been stripped on stage, and he called that decent?

"But I'm not done with you for tonight. I have a promise to keep, and you're going to help me keep it."

She knew she hadn't been given permission to talk, but since it was just the two of them now, she couldn't help herself. "What promise?"

"If she got you off, I'd get her off."

Again, Kylie's eyes widened. "We need to talk about this sharing thing. I'm not okay with watching you go down on some other chick. I don't like the idea of you with anyone else."

One side of Freddie's mouth kicked up into a grin. "Jealousy, Kylie? I wasn't expecting that. You invested in me now, sweetheart?"

Before she could answer, he cut her to the quick with his next statement. "Because I've got to say, I just loved watching you and Josh suck face at every party we went to the year you two went out."

Josh was a friend of X and Freddie's, one she'd dated the year after graduating high school. If she remembered correctly, Freddie hadn't been around all that much. He'd been off at university learning how to code and how to perfect his artwork. But apparently, he remembered that year.

Hannah was right. Darrell was right. There was no way things from that long ago would bother him if he wasn't interested in her. She could win that spot in his bed. Her gaze darted to the bar where Angel was tossing back a shot. She just had to get through whatever he had in mind for tonight.

She glanced back at him. "So what is this, payback?"

He placed her on the bench beside him before removing himself from the booth. He placed one hand on the back of the bench and the other on the table, caging her in. "Tell me, Kylie, did you ever even come when you were with him? Did he ever make you cream like you did the other night for me?"

Kylie felt her face go red. Her body started to throb all over again, remembering the way he'd gotten her off last week.

"I had to get those pants dry cleaned, you know." His hand left the table and darted between her thighs. He dragged a finger along her lips, pushing the fabric against her. "Did he ever make your pussy feel as good as I do?"

She blinked, her gaze locked on his. She wanted to demand he take her home, to make her feel that way again and again, to make her forget about every woman he'd ever touched and forget about every man who'd ever failed her.

"Answer me, Kylie."

"No." The word slipped out. She cleared her throat before giving him another dose of honesty. "No one has."

"Then, you need to trust me." He nodded to the corner of the booth. "Shift over. You're going to help me fulfill my promise to Angel."

She wanted to object, but she'd gotten snagged on those words. Trust me.

When Angel arrived back at his booth, Kylie sat quietly as instructed, wondering what dirty, filthy thing Freddie would have her do next.

Freddie moved aside and let Angel claim the space next to her.

Rather boldly, Angel told her, "You taste pretty good, but not as good as a Christmas cookie shot. Wanna try?"

Before Kylie could question it, Angel wrapped her hand in her hair and pulled her mouth toward her own. For a sub, Angel certainly didn't kiss like one. She was controlling and dominating in the way she used her lips, her tongue, and her teeth. She didn't let Kylie go, firmly holding her in place.

She pushed a little closer, and Kylie realized Freddie had squeezed into the booth as well.

Kylie felt his hand grab hers beneath the table. Together, their joined hands slid up beneath Angel's miniskirt, answering Kylie's questions about what would happen. Freddie's big hand directed hers, pulling her index finger free and using it to push aside the panel of Angel's panties.

The woman was already wet, the space between her legs warm and ripe as Freddie led Kylie's finger through her folds, up against her clit, and then back down. Using his index finger as well as her own, he inserted them into Angel's pussy. The redhead arched off the bench. The hand she used to anchor Kylie's head was suddenly shaking.

So, she wasn't as in control as she seemed to think. She had a weakness for Freddie and the things he could do, just like pretty well every woman in the club.

Freddie used their joined fingers to fuck the woman between them. Over and over, they plowed into her, rolling with her momentum as she chased the same type of climax Kylie had just enjoyed.

She tore her mouth away from Kylie's and turned in favor of Freddie, clutching at his shirt, trying to pull him closer, trying to claim his mouth. "Please, Santa, please."

Kylie watched as Freddie's lips curved into a smile. He obviously loved the power exchange and how he could manipulate this woman and bend her to his will. Kylie could feel her finger being gripped tighter and tighter. The smell of sex lingered in the air.

"Santa, please!" Her cries became more and more desperate, more frantic.

Freddie removed his finger from the woman's passage, pulling Kylie's out as well. He pressed three of her fingers together and brought them back to her entrance. "Don't stop until I tell you to."

A little in awe of what was happening at the dark transformation in Freddie, Kylie did as she was told and pumped her hand once more against the woman, shoving three fingers in deep only to drag them out and do it again.

Angel squirmed, coming further and further undone.

Freddie grabbed a fist full of her hair and pinned her head back against the bench. "Did you enjoy tongue fucking my sub, you naughty little angel?"

The noise Angel made wasn't coherent. Her head continued to thrash.

"Answer me, or you don't come yet." His grip tightened, and all Angel's movements stopped.

Tears were forming in the corners of her eyes. "You promised."

"You'll get your orgasm, but I say when. Answer me, or I'll have you begging to fuck her again just so you can come."

Kylie couldn't help that her breaths were coming in pants. What the fuck was happening to her? She was wet again, so wet she knew she could take Freddie without any prep. And when had that ever been the case? His words were harsh, pushy, and demanding, yet Kylie knew both of them—she and Angel—would do anything he said at that moment.

Angel wet her lips. "What was the question again?" Her body bucked against Kylie's hand.

"Did you enjoy putting your tongue in my sub's sweet little cunt?"

"Oh my God," Kylie breathed. For the first time since he'd

taken control, Freddie's gaze switched over to her. His jaw was hard, his stare unforgiving.

"Yes. Yes!" Angel cried. "I loved it. Let me come now, please."

Freddie's hand dipped below the table again, his fingers rubbing on Angel's clit. "Faster, Kylie, fuck her faster."

She didn't realize her tempo had slowed as she witnessed their conversation. She followed his order and increased her speed.

Between them, Angel writhed until suddenly her body tensed, and her pussy gripped Kylie's fingers hard, spasming around her. As the orgasm lifted, Kylie began to remove her hand, but Freddie's voice halted her. "Did I tell you to stop?"

"No," she answered.

"Keep going." His command was unnecessary. She was already shoving her fingers back in.

"No, Santa, please," Angel begged, her tune changing.

His fingers moved quickly over her clit, pushing her hard and fast to a second climax. "Is this what you wanted? What you begged me for?"

"Ah, God!" Angel's face was covered in tears, her hair a mess.

"I promised if you made her scream, I'd make you scream." Freddie's fingers moved relentlessly, making Kylie wish he'd touch her soon. "You haven't screamed yet."

It was only a matter of moments before Angel's scream ripped through the club.

Nearby, someone clapped.

Angel collapsed against the seat, sagging after her release. Freddie placed a kiss to her hair. She looked up at him with a satisfied smile on her lips. "Your newest trainee isn't half bad, Sir."

Kylie paused. Newest trainee. As in, not the first and not the last. She shook her head. She'd just helped him get another woman off. What was wrong with her? Where was her self-respect? She was making it too easy for him.

"Excuse me." Kylie didn't bother to wait for them to move. After all the intimate things she'd just done, she practically crawled over them to escape the booth.

Soon, she was speed-walking through the club. She dipped

into the bathroom to clean herself up before washing her hands. She needed them to smell like soap, not Angel's pussy. She scrubbed for longer than she needed to before exiting the washroom and headed for the coatroom.

With her coat wrapped around her elf costume and the belt pulled tight, she all but ran from the club.

"Kylie, wait!" Freddie's voice stopped her from hailing a cab.

He closed the gap between them in three long strides, yanked her into his arms, and kissed her. His tongue slid across her lip, demanding entrance, which she quickly granted. Way too easily.

"God, I've wanted to do that all night," he told her as they parted.

But he'd waited until they were away from prying eyes, just like he had the week before. Maybe it wasn't done publicly, but he was definitely showing her favoritism. She wasn't sure what to say. Luckily, Freddie wasn't done.

"No more sharing. I'm finished letting anyone else touch you."

Kylie blinked. What about those that touched him? Was that finished, too, or was she hoping for too much?

"Promise?"

"Yes."

Kylie hugged her coat a little tighter. "Well, at least I know you keep your promises."

Freddie let out a laugh. "That I do." He stepped closer. "From now on, no one touches your body but me." With one hand, he ran his thumb over her lower lip; with the other, he used to wave down a cab. "I'll see you on Saturday."

The Christmas party. She'd almost forgotten about it. They'd both be attending. How the fuck was that going to work?

Chapter Seven

"I don't know why I'm so nervous," Kylie whispered to Hannah so Janet couldn't hear her. Even two rooms away, Janet's ability to eavesdrop was about as legendary as her snooping skills.

Hannah dumped a bag of chips into a bowl. "I'm excited. I want to see what he's like outside the club. I want to see this nice guy you keep talking about. I've only ever seen the bossy bastard in a Santa suit."

"Hush!" Kylie warned. "If Janet finds out..."

"You need to chill, girl," Hannah said with a laugh. "He's not going to do or say anything crazy."

"I'm more worried about how I'll be around him." She leaned closer. "I can't seem to control myself. I'm not going to be able to think about anything else."

"You mean like how he got you to finger fuck his last sub?"

Kylie nudged her. "Shut up."

Hannah's laughter trailed after her as she rounded the counter with the bowl of chips. "It was hot."

"What was hot?" Janet walked into the kitchen.

Unable to think of an answer, Kylie stood immobile while Hannah gave a perfect reply. "This guy that comes into the gym. He's smoking hot. Real badass, too."

Janet smiled before reaching inside the fridge to pull out the first veggie tray. "I bet you there's a lot of hot guys that come into the gym. You must be floating in hot man soup."

Hannah set the bowl on the dining room table and returned for a tray filled with M&Ms and pretzels. "You're a photographer at a fashion magazine. Talk about hot guy soup! I'm surprised you haven't tried to hook Kylie up with one of those sexy models."

"I've thought about it." Janet giggled. "She needs to get laid."

"What?" Shocked, Kylie thought her eyes might just pop out of their sockets.

"Oh, come on!" Janet smacked her on the arm as she walked past with a big sleeve of plastic cups. "You've been so surly lately. There's only one cure for that."

"Amen!" Hannah said, around a crunchy pretzel.

Kylie glared at her friend, who only shrugged in response, a smile curving her lips.

"By the way," Janet said while grabbing a few bottle openers from the drawer and laying them on the counter next to the wine and liquor bottles. "The first guests are arriving. Can you get the door?"

Kylie disappeared down the front hallway, eager to see *him*, but disappointment flooded her when she realized it was a few of Janet's friends from the magazine, as well as X's secretary. She faked a smile and opened the door wide with a pleasant greeting. Each one came with a can or boxed good, as requested. Every person invited was to bring something for the charity food drive Janet volunteered at during the holidays.

"Not him?" Hannah murmured, looking over the party guests as she joined Kylie at the door. Her tone reflected Kylie's disappointment.

"I don't know why I thought he'd be the first one here. He never is." She shook her head. "I need to get it together."

Despite saying so, Kylie knew she wouldn't be able to. Whenever the doorbell rang, she either rushed to answer it or had to glance over to check if it was him. Each time, it was someone else.

As the house began to fill with people, Kylie finally started to unwind. She held a cooler in her hand and chatted with a group of people she remembered from last year when she heard his voice.

Attempting not to seem too eager, she excused herself from the group and approached the entrance. There he was, wiping snow from his hair while balancing an armful of items.

"Can I help you with something?" Janet asked.

His smile was kind and friendly. Freddie's typical smile. "Thanks." He passed her a few of the items before pulling off his coat.

"My, my." Hannah's breath was at her ear. Kylie glanced over, unsure of where Hannah had popped up from. "He looks even better than he does at the club."

Kylie prayed that neither Janet nor Freddie heard her over the music. There was no indication that they had. She had to agree that Freddie looked fine in what was no doubt tailored dress pants and a button-up light green collared shirt. His sleeves were rolled up, revealing muscular forearms, and when he turned to hang up his coat, they all got a chance to view his specular ass in those tight pants. The impression of his wallet was in the back pocket, but it didn't deter from the sight.

What woman wouldn't want to rip off his clothes, drop to her knees, and offer him anything he wanted in exchange for his touch?

He took back the items from Janet, but he passed her a bottle of wine. "This is for you. Make sure you hide it and save it for yourself," he instructed.

Janet clutched the bottle to her chest, swaying back and forth. "My favorite!"

Freddie chuckled. "And I didn't have time to grab a can, but I hope this makes up for it." From his pocket, he pulled out a small, folded piece of paper.

Taking the cheque from him, Janet shook her head. She glanced down at the amount. "Freddie, you really didn't have to."

He gave a schoolboy-type shrug. "It's the holidays."

"Yeah, but twelve grand..." Janet complained about the generous amount.

Hannah whistled in shock.

"Will help get the shelter through the holidays and give them a good start on next year," Freddie finished the thought for Janet.

Shaking her head, Janet went on tiptoe and kissed his cheek. "Thank you for this."

He gave her a half hug. "Not a problem. Is it okay if I tuck this under the tree for safekeeping? The future owner isn't here yet, and I don't want to keep it with me." He pointed to the last item in his hands, a box wrapped in a similar ribbon as the one he'd had delivered to the gym.

Hannah nudged Kylie.

"Of course," Janet told him.

"Great." He toed off his dress shoes. "Anything I can help with in the kitchen?"

Janet waved him away. "No, thanks. Here, I can take that, too." She took the little box from him and disappeared down the hall.

"Kylie." For the first time, Freddie's gaze fell on her. He nodded in her direction. "And it was Hannah, right?"

He held out a hand in greeting, pretending like he hadn't seen Hannah at the club two days before.

"Yep, Hannah." She let him shake her hand. "You know, you look familiar..."

Kylie elbowed her friend. "Stop."

With a laugh, Hannah trotted off. "I'm going to go get wasted."

Kylie took a deep breath, her gaze swinging from her friend to Freddie. "So, how does this work?"

Freddie's eyes narrowed ever so slightly. "The same way it always has. It's a party. We drink, we eat, we socialize."

"Right." Kylie took a sip from her drink, thankful for the distraction.

He leaned down just a bit. "Unless you have another idea on how to pass the time."

Kylie choked and covered her mouth with her hand.

He was smiling as he strode off, taking the same path to the kitchen as Janet had.

She wasn't sure what would happen as the night progressed, but it sure as hell wouldn't be the same as last year.

The party was nothing like last year.

Last year, she'd been drinking, chatting, and enjoying her single life.

This year, she was pulled in two directions. Part of her wanted to follow Freddie around, watch him, and see how he behaved; the other wanted to hide. She didn't want anyone to guess how her feelings about him had changed.

From the outside, his behavior seemed no different than in previous years, but for her, everything was different. So many of his comments could be taken and twisted to make them dirty. Nearly any time she conversed with him, he seemed to be dropping hints or deliberately saying things to try and get a rise out of her.

And it was working. Her panties were soaked—from his words, from the smell of his cologne, from the memories of everything that had transpired between them over the last few weeks.

Every time she was in the living room, she couldn't help but glance at the little box that sat beneath the tree. Was it for her? And what was in it?

She scrubbed a hand over her face, trying to get a grip on her lust.

"Too much to drink?" Freddie asked as he plopped down beside her on the loveseat. Nearby, people were scattered around the room. Four were playing Mario Kart on the Switch, and two were huddled in the corner, swaying to the music and trying not to lean toward one another. Another few people sat on nearby furniture or the floor, chatting about work and families. A game of euchre was happening in the dining room, and in the den, the hockey game was on. Periodically, the crowd from the den would shout, cheer, or collectively groan.

"No." Kylie took another sip from her bottle. "This is only my second cooler."

"You look troubled." His arm dropped over the back of the seat, his fingers casually grazing her hair before tapping along the leather. It would seem innocent to anyone else, but for Kylie, it was all too personal.

"Tired, maybe," she tried to come up with an excuse.

"She needs to get laid." This time, the voice came from Hannah, who knelt by the coffee table doing shots.

"I could help with that," Josh, who'd been playing Mario Cart, pipped up. Kylie hated that he was here, but he was still a friend of X's.

She didn't bother responding to him but rolled her eyes. There was no way she'd be letting Josh touch her ever again. He'd left her colder than the Arctic and lacked any type of real skill when it came to sex.

"Even her sister agrees," Hannah said, completely embarrassing Kylie.

"Oh, my God." She put her face in her hands, trying to cover her blush.

Emmett, the model who had been following Janet around most of the night but had recently given up his efforts in favor of trying to seduce one of the nurses who worked at the hospital with X, stopped trying to toss M&M's in the air and catch them with his mouth. "I've got some friends I could hook you up with." He dug his phone out of his pocket. "I can even give you a little preview. You can pick the one you like best. What's your poison? Tall, short, bald, facial hair, tattoos?"

"Ooh, let me see!" Hannah squealed and hoisted herself off the floor and into the vacant seat next to Emmett.

Freddie smiled and shook his head at their antics, but as they glanced through Emmett's phone, Freddie leaned closer and whispered in her ear, "You even think about letting another man touch you, and I'll spank your pussy until you're dripping and begging for my cock."

Her face went redder. She could feel the blood rushing to it.

Her vaginal muscles clamped tightly. She couldn't take much more.

"This one is cute!" Hannah turned the phone toward her.

Kylie glanced at the phone, but for the life of her, she couldn't focus. Draining the rest of the bottle, she shoved up from the couch. "Time for another."

She made her way to the kitchen, dropped off her empty, and headed to the laundry room.

Stepping inside, she gripped the washing machine and took a deep breath. This is what she needed: space and quiet. She needed a moment to think, to gather herself, and to stop the ache between her legs.

Everything he said was either outright naughty or sounded sexual to her ears, with dirty promises and flirty innuendos. She knew he did it on purpose to rile her, and it was working. She was just lucky that Janet or X hadn't pieced it together yet.

She'd never wanted a man as much as she wanted Freddie. And just how had he done that? Two weeks ago, he was her brother's friend, a nice guy. Now he was the dirty son of a bitch who made her do unspeakable things just for a chance at his cock. When had she become such a slut?

Just then, the door opened, light from the other room invading her hiding place. Freddie flashed her a grin. "Running from me?"

Determined not to cower, she straightened.

He shut the door, letting the darkness envelop them.

Her skin burned for his touch, but he flicked on the light instead. She blinked up at him. Had he always been this tall?

He stepped closer. "Or were you hoping I'd follow you here?"

Had she hoped that? Suddenly, she wasn't sure why she'd walked into this room. To escape? Or so he could make good on his naughty, dirty promises?

"I'm not in the habit of giving chase." He took another step forward.

She backed up, her legs hitting the washing machine. "Yet here you are."

"I'm curious." His head tilted to the side. "Are you here because I said something to make you uncomfortable? Or because your pussy is seeping, and you just couldn't take it anymore?"

Her pulse tripled. She wanted Freddie to find out for himself —wanted him to put his fingers inside her and rub until she came.

With his hand, he cupped her chin, those deep green eyes trying to read her very soul, it seemed. His thumb passed along her lower lip. "Tell me."

She tried not to lick his thumb. "The second one."

He leaned closer and whispered in her ear, "Say the words."

Closing her eyes, she was about to speak when he covered her lips with his thumb.

"No. Eyes open. Don't be a coward. Look at me."

Swallowing hard, she glanced up. He didn't smile. His face was firm, his gaze direct, commanding, and so different from the softness she witnessed when he talked with everyone else throughout the night.

Uttering a few dirty words was nothing compared to the other things she'd already done simply because he'd asked. Summoning what courage she could, she told him, "Yes. I'm wet."

He laughed. "Oh, come now. You can do better than that."

She blushed.

When all this was said and done, when it came time to choose who would sub for him in less than a week's time, would he pick her? Was she guaranteed a spot in his bed? Or did he make all his potential subs burn for him?

She drew a deep breath before the words came spilling out. "I'm so wet, I'm dripping. My panties are sticking to my pussy, and it's so uncomfortable, and all I can think about is your cock."

"Good girl." His murmured praise vibrated along her skin as his lips skimmed her neck.

Her body sagged. Those two little words made all the difference. He was pleased.

His thumb pressed against her lips once more, this time demanding entrance. She parted them and drew the digit into her mouth. She wrapped her tongue around it, sucked hard, then did it again. She placed her hand on his chest and could feel the rise and fall of his chest as her sucking action made his breath grow faster.

"Look at me," he commanded.

She did, glancing at him while his thick thumb was still in her mouth.

"Fuck, that's hot," he muttered. "You told me you want to be fucked hard, to be used up, to be completely spent and at a man's total mercy."

Yes, she'd said those things the first night she saw him at the club. She'd been shocked by his presence and wanted to shock him right back. But though she'd been trying to surprise him, they were still truthful words—every single one.

She nodded.

"If that's what you want, then you're going to get on your knees, take out my cock and suck it. You're going to take it as deep as you can, and then, when that's not enough for me, I'm going to take over."

Her nostrils flared with her indrawn breath. The idea of him taking control during a blowjob both terrified her and turned her on even more.

He removed his thumb and snapped his fingers. "Knees, now."

She dropped, fumbled with his belt and pants, but finally succeeded in getting his dick out. It was magnificent, long and thick, making her wonder how she'd take it all.

Grabbing her hands, he directed them to his thighs. "Only use your mouth," he instructed.

Moving up a bit, she took him into her mouth. At first, she just sucked lightly on the tip, getting used to his taste, his smell. She circled the thick head before taking a little more. She could feel him holding himself back, letting her take the lead. Occasionally, he'd rock forward, but then he'd stop, allowing her to stay in charge of the tempo, the depth.

"Look up at me."

Her gaze swept upward, and she could just imagine what he saw. A woman, on her knees, worshiping his body with her mouth.

She clenched her thighs together to try to ease the ache she felt there.

He pushed in a little deeper, making her take more than she previously had. Was this it? Was he going to take over now? How did she prepare for such a thing? She'd never deep-throated anyone before.

She didn't get a chance to find out.

Suddenly, the door opened, and Janet strode through. "Kylie, why are you—" Her words died on her tongue.

Kylie pulled away and glanced around Freddie's legs to see the shock in her sister's eyes. Her mouth was open in alarm as she stood there, paused in the doorway. Without another word, Janet pulled the door shut. Her hurried footsteps rushed away from the room.

"Oh, my God!" Kylie whispered. "That was awful." She tried to stand, but Freddie stopped her with a hard hand on her shoulder.

"Where do you think you're going?"

"I have to go after her." She motioned to the closed door. "I have to talk to her."

"No, you have to finish what you started."

She blinked up at him. "You can't be serious. Not after what just happened."

"If you want to be crossed off the naughty list, you can leave. You know where the door is." He motioned with his head to the space where Janet had been just seconds before. "But if you want a shot at learning what it's really like to be a sub, what it's really like to spend a night in my bed, aching and screaming in pleasure, you'll stay on your knees and open your fucking mouth."

Her pussy gushed. Conflicted tears welled in her eyes.

"I won't wait. You have five seconds to decide."

She bit her lip. Would Janet be okay for a few more minutes?

"Five. Four."

Kylie glanced up at Freddie, still fully clothed with his dick erect, reaching out toward her. She almost couldn't believe how unrelenting he was, considering the current situation.

"Three. Two."

If he got to one, she knew he wouldn't wait. He'd tuck himself away and rejoin the party. He'd be done with her.

Before he could speak the last digit, Kylie opened her mouth wide and leaned forward.

"Good girl." She barely heard his muttered praise because his cock was right there, shoving into her mouth. His hand encased the back of her head as he thrust inside. Her jaw opened wider as he thrust again and again, each time going deeper than the last. "Good fucking girl."

He grunted as he penetrated her mouth, his rapid plunges pushing the head of his cock into her throat.

Tears slipped free from the corner of her eyes as she attempted to breathe through her nose.

Panting, he stopped. His dark gaze bore into her as she knelt by his feet. He only gave her a moment to catch her breath before saying, "Again."

He pulled her to him, drawing her mouth down his cock, until he was so far down her throat that she thought she'd gag.

"Swallow around it." He held her there for a moment.

Pulling back again, he continued thrusting, this time with more shallow thrusts before a deeper one. He repeated the process, this time telling her how good she felt, how pleased he was. Each word, each shove of his cock made her pussy pulse with need. She wanted to be the one he chose, the only woman on his list.

"You're such a dirty girl, Kylie. I've wanted you for a long time, but I knew you didn't want me. You didn't want the man who treated you kindly. But now that I'm treating you like a well-used whore, you're happy to suck my cock, aren't you? You'd let me put it where I wanted, wouldn't you?"

She couldn't answer, but she mumbled anyway. Right now, she'd do anything he asked as long as he continued to make her feel sexy and alive in ways she never had before.

"You wanted a man to use you up. To take his pleasure from you. How do you like it now, Kylie? How do you like it with my dick shoved down your throat?"

Her hips began to rock. She needed him inside her so, so badly.

His hands shook as his fingers dug into her hair, tugging slightly. "I'm going to come, Kylie. I'm going to come, and you're going to drink it down."

That was all the warning she got. He held her head steady and trust into her two, three more times, and then he blew. He pulsed against her tongue as she drank down his cum. She could hear his labored breaths as he pulled away.

Sitting back on her heels, she tried to catch her breath. She licked her lips. Her body was still primed and pulsing. When had she become this sex-crazed vixen?

"I'm not leaving the party," he told her. "It would be suspicious. You're going to have to put up with seeing me here for another few hours. You should probably go speak with your sister." He zipped himself back up. "She's probably a little shocked."

A little?

He pulled her to her feet. With her hands still clasped in his, she thought he might drag her in for a kiss, but instead, he lifted her fingers and pressed his lips to the pad of one. "You'll probably want a drink now, too."

She smiled. "Something strong, I think."

He laughed, but then his grip and his demeanor changed as he drew her finger inside his mouth and sucked it hard. Kylie whimpered. He released her in favor of grasping the doorknob. "Tonight, when you're lying in bed fucking yourself with your dildo, pretend it's me."

Kylie opened her mouth to speak, but he was gone.

As if she wasn't already planning on thinking of him.

Chapter Eight

Janet was in the living room doing shots with Emmett and a few of the writers from the magazine when Kylie found her. Her gaze was filled with distaste, but she didn't say a word.

When they poured their next round of shots, Kylie grabbed Janet's before she had a chance to. Not caring what was in the glass, Kylie tossed it back.

Tequila. Yep, strong.

She set the glass on the table and looked at Janet. "Can we talk?"

"Are you sure? I thought you were busy. I didn't want to interrupt you when you had your mouth full."

Trying not to let shame and embarrassment show on her face, she growled, "Now."

Emmett glanced back and forth between them, clearly entertained by the tension. Kylie didn't miss the fact that his hand was resting on the small of Janet's back, dangerously close to her ass.

Janet rolled her eyes but heaved herself off the couch and muttered, "Where do you want to talk? Because I'm not going back to that laundry room."

"Upstairs." Kylie started in that direction.

They'd barely reached the upstairs hallway when Janet started. "So, is this a fling or what?"

Kylie drew up short at the question. She didn't know what was going on between her and Freddie, but she knew she couldn't give her sister any actual details. She shrugged. "I don't know what it is."

"What are you thinking? What is X going to think?"

"Oh, please. He's not going to care." She walked a few steps away. "We've both dated friends of his."

"Yeah, but not his best friend. What if he'd been the one to walk in on you tonight and saw what I saw?" Then, as though reliving it, she rubbed her eyes and chanted, "Get out. Get out. Get out."

Kylie placed a hand on her sister's arm. "I'm really sorry you walked in on that. I got caught up in the moment. But come on, you can't have seen that much." At most, she'd have seen Kylie on her knees and Freddie's backside. She doubted his ass would have even been bare.

"I saw enough."

"Maybe it's not what it looked like."

Janet gave her a slanted 'yeah, right' look. "What? Was his zipper broken, and you were trying to fix it with your teeth?"

Kylie couldn't help but giggle. Okay, maybe there weren't a lot of reasons why she'd be on her knees in front of him.

"This isn't funny, Kylie. How could you seduce Freddie? He's practically family. He grew up with us!"

"Whoa!" Frowning, Kylie held up her hand. She didn't know which part of that to address first. She wasn't seducing anyone. "He lived with us for like six months after the accident, and he was what? Eighteen at the time? That's hardly growing up with us." Silence stretched between them until Kylie broke it. "It's really not any of your business anyway."

Her sister looked hurt, but it was the truth. Whatever Kylie had with Freddie wasn't a family decision. She had no business being involved.

Crossing her arms over her chest, Janet frowned. "Look, I know everyone thinks I'm a busybody and a snoop." She sighed. "I can't help the way I am. But I'm legitimately worried about this, Kylie. Freddie is special. One of a kind."

She has no idea, Kylie thought.

"And while I'm sure that's tempting, I mean, he's a really sweet guy, but he doesn't even live in this country for most of the year. He's off working in the States. What kind of future is there?"

Kylie had already been wondering that herself, but she didn't bother validating Janet's question. "Maybe that's not what this is about. Maybe it's just fun." She thought back to Emmett in the living room. "And maybe that's something you should consider."

Janet's eyebrow rose. "Having casual sex with Freddie?"

"No." Kylie couldn't help but laugh again. "Emmett."

Janet lifted her arms in exasperation. "I told you, nothing is going on with him."

"Really?" Kylie lifted a brow. "Because you looked awful cozy on the couch just now."

Janet narrowed her eyes. "Nothing is going on."

Kylie raised her hands in front of her as though she was defending herself. "If you say so. It's none of my business, just like what's happening with me is none of yours."

Her sister's nostrils flared. "I—"

Janet's words were cut off when they heard the sound of someone throwing up in a nearby washroom. The sisters glanced at each other before heading in that direction.

Another hurling sound was accompanied by Freddie's voice. "You'll feel better once you've gotten it out of your system."

The door was slightly ajar, so Kylie pressed her palm to it and nudged it open. Freddie sat on the side of the tub with his knees bent at an odd angle to accommodate Hannah, who knelt gripping the toilet. He rubbed her back with one hand, and with the other, he held her hair in a loose ponytail so she wouldn't throw up on it.

He glanced up at the intrusion. "Do either of you have a hair tie?"

"Of course." Janet left in a hurry, moving toward her bedroom.

Cautiously, Kylie stepped into the small room. "Hannah, are you okay?"

Her friend gave a slight nod, but she didn't look up from the toilet. "Yep. I just mixed too many drinks. I'm going to be in so much trouble. I was supposed to meet them later tonight."

"Who's them?" Kylie asked.

Freddie slanted her a look.

"Oh!" Her Doms. Yeah, this probably wouldn't go over well.

With his hand on her back, Freddie told her, "It'll be okay. Don't dwell on that now."

"Right." Hannah nodded. "Priorities. Get the room to stop spinning first."

He chuckled.

Janet returned with a hairband. After fastening Hannah's hair into a loose ponytail, Freddie pulled out his phone.

Kylie's brow furrowed as she watched him take care of her friend. All of a sudden, the books she read came flooding back to her. All those sexy Doms who made their woman come so hard she screamed and trembled. They'd all been good at something else, too. Aftercare.

The way Freddie was so gentle and kind, holding Hannah's hair and then tying it back, made Kylie realize just how the two sides of him fit together. Most men would have passed her the tie. Hell, most wouldn't have stopped to help at all. They would have found her or Janet and sent them. But not Freddie. He cared about people.

He tucked his phone back into his pocket.

"How are you feeling now?" Janet asked.

"Stupid," came Hannah's reply. "I'm not some freshman who can't hold her liquor." She spat into the porcelain bowl before wiping her mouth with toilet paper and flushing everything down.

"No," Freddie said, "but those Jell-o shots were strong, and you had a good amount of them."

"They tasted so good." Hannah repositioned herself, plopping down on her butt rather than her knees. "At least on the way down."

"I'm going to get you some water," Janet told her.

"And a bucket, if you have one," Freddie interjected before Janet could leave. "I've called for a ride for her, but my driver will be pissed if she throws up in the car."

"A driver?" Kylie asked.

"Thank you." Hannah leaned her head against his knee.

Absentmindedly, it seemed, he began stroking her head. "A local guy I sometimes use when I'm in town if I don't want to or can't drive myself."

Kylie's gaze was locked on where he patted Hannah's hair. "You always have such fancy cars when you come here, though."

He nodded. "Most of the time, yes. I prefer to drive myself. I like cars as much as the next guy, but sometimes I'm at a function where it's impractical, or I decide to work during the ride."

Working in the car? Yep, this was yet another side of Freddie she never saw. The businessman. Sure, she knew he was a multi-millionaire. He lavished them with gifts; he loaned them money to buy their house; he gave big cheques to small charities, but the man behind all that, the one who made the money, who worked hard? That man she didn't know.

There was so much more to him than the pushover she'd once thought he was. Suddenly, she wished she could be a fly on the wall in his office, to see what he did on a daily basis, to see how he handled himself.

It was the first time she'd thought about visiting him in the States, that she'd considered the possibility of a relationship between them.

But then again, did he have subs he kept in the States?

Her focus narrowed on his hand. With each stroke over Hannah's crown, Kylie wondered where he usually took his pleasure. Surely, December at the club wasn't the extent of his BDSM activities.

Soon, Janet returned with a bottle of water and a bucket. It took about five minutes before Hannah felt well enough to stand without throwing up, and once she could, they were all headed for the door. Kylie helped her friend, and Janet carried the water bottle for her. Freddie tagged along behind them.

When they walked her out to the waiting town car, Janet stayed inside to check on the other guests and quickly cleaned the bathroom. Kylie helped her friend into the car.

"Are you going to be okay with going home alone?" She didn't like the idea of her friend being on her own.

"I'll be okay. The worst is passed, I think. I just want to sleep now."

"Yeah, but I still feel like you shouldn't be on your own. Maybe you should stay here tonight."

"She's not going home."

Both women turned to look at Freddie. "What?"

"She's going to Darrell's place."

"What?" This time, it was Hannah who squeaked.

Freddie leaned closer to the car, keeping his voice low. "Your Doms were expecting you tonight. Your phone fell out of your pocket when you were sick, and I let them know the situation. They said to send you to Darrell's. They'll want to take care of you. Let them."

"Fine." Hannah huffed but relented. "Thank you. Though I probably won't be so thankful tomorrow."

Freddie grinned, flashing a dimple. "Oh, I'm sure you'll be thankful then, too."

Hannah chuckled as she slid further into the backseat.

As the car drove off, Kylie turned to Freddie. "Why will she be thankful tomorrow?"

"Tomorrow night or the next day, depending on how she's feeling." Freddie glanced at her before heading back to the house. "She'll be punished for drinking too much."

"Punished?" Kylie kept up with his long-legged stride.

Turning to her, he stopped. "Yes, punished." He shifted closer to her. "And she'll love every second of it. Just like you will when my palm finally connects with that sexy little ass of yours."

Kylie paused on the driveway.

He looked again toward the house before gently nudging her

into the shadowy area by the garage. Glancing up with wide eyes, she followed his lead until she was backed up against the brick.

"You still wet for me?"

She groaned as his hand found its way between her open coat panels and cupped her breast through her sweater. "Yes. Always it seems."

He ground his pelvis against hers as his hand wrapped in her hair. "I'm hard again already. I shouldn't be, seeing as I came down your throat not half an hour ago."

With a moan, she clutched at his jacket and pulled him closer. It wasn't his warmth she was seeking but his lips. They came down atop hers, his tongue stealing into her mouth as though it belonged there. And maybe it did.

What would it be like to be Freddie's? Not just for a night but longer. Maybe even for always?

Groaning, he gathered her closer. She enjoyed the wicked sweep of his tongue, the way he lightly bit her lower lip.

When he pulled away, she felt the cold rushing back in. "Please..." she whispered without opening her eyes. She wanted more. Needed more.

"No, Kylie." His tone, not quite as sharp as normal, drew her attention. She looked up into those gorgeous green eyes, into that perfectly sculpted face. "Not tonight. But soon."

She rubbed her thighs together, trying to ease the ache he caused. She wanted to beg him for release, but she knew it wouldn't do her any good. His control was too hard, his patience too strong.

"Do you want to come tonight?"

Her gaze widened. "Like to your place?" Was he really going to break his rule?

He laughed. "No." Cupping her cheeks, he grinned down at her. "I fucking love how eager you are."

She blushed, though she couldn't help feeling desperate for him. And frankly, a little disappointed.

"I meant come as in orgasm. As in me pushing you so close to the edge that you're dripping, and you come so hard the only thing on your mind will be how badly you want me."

Her lips parted on an exhale. "Yes."

"Tonight. You'll do as I instruct. And if you're a good girl, then next week, you'll be coming with that hot little cunt wrapped around my dick."

Confused and dumbfounded.

That's how Kylie felt when Freddie said goodbye to X and left for the night—his promise left unfulfilled.

She figured they'd sneak away again, that he'd get her off, and they'd return to the party like nothing had happened, but instead, he'd left. Then she remembered his order from when they'd been in the laundry room, the one for her to use her vibrator and think of him. Was that what she was supposed to do? It seemed a little anti-climactic.

She wandered through the living room, glancing toward the tree, but the little gift he'd brought with him was gone. Had that not been for her?

As the night wound down, all she wanted to do was go to her room and lock the door, but unfortunately, after the last guest left, Janet insisted they clean up some of the mess. With their brother passed out on the couch, she and Janet went around him collecting plastic cups, real glasses, and empty beer bottles. Once they had everything placed in the kitchen and all the food packaged up, Janet finally relented and allowed Kylie to go to bed.

In the bathroom, she quickly brushed and flossed her teeth before heading to her room. With the door locked, she pulled off her sweater and started tugging on her pants. That's when she noticed the gift on her bed. The little box from beneath the tree had somehow made its way into her room.

Was that why Freddie had been upstairs when Hannah started throwing up?

She glanced at the tag, which read,

From Santa.

Her heart fluttered. Desperate to see what was inside, she finished stripping, grabbed her vibrator from the chest in her closet, and hopped onto the bed. She made quick work of the ribbon and tore open the lid. She had to dump the contents before figuring out what it was.

It looked a bit like a dog collar, but the bright red ball in the middle gave away its true purpose.

It was a ball gag. He'd left a ball gag on her bed. Why that made her wetter than she already was, she didn't know.

Her attention drifted to the small note which had floated out when she emptied the box:

Put in your vibrator. Turn it on to the lowest setting. Put on the gag. Call me immediately.

With shaky hands, she picked up the gag to inspect it. Would he really want her to call him after two AM?

Tonight, things had gotten real. They'd gotten intimate. It was no longer about pushing her limits in public. It was about them. She was sure he would select her to be his sub next week, but images of other women on his lap, of him touching and kissing other subs, even after seeing her at the club, bothered her. She didn't want to risk his wrath, though; she didn't want to risk not being picked.

Still wet from earlier in the evening and even damper now that she held his gag, Kylie reclined on the bed, inserted her vibrator, and turned it on as instructed. Next, she grabbed the gag. She popped it in her mouth and carefully fastened it behind her head. It was tricky, and with shaky nerves, it took her a few tries. By the time she was finished, it was probably looser than he would have liked, but it would do the trick.

She took her phone from the nightstand, called his number,

and put it on speakerphone. With the volume turned low, she doubted anyone would hear it. It was likely Janet was asleep, and X was still downstairs snoring.

After three rings, he picked up. "Hello?"

She didn't respond. She didn't know that she could, with her mouth stuffed full.

"I expected you to call earlier. Did Janet make you clean up first?"

Still, she made no noise.

"You're going to want to answer me. I need to know it's you and that you're alone before we begin."

Begin? Begin what?

Her heart thumped hard against her ribs. God, he excited her.

She mumbled a response.

"Excellent." He sounded pleased. "Is your pussy full? Is it wet?"

Kylie squeezed her eyes shut. How could he jump right into it like that? She made a weak reply through the gag.

"I won't ask you any more questions, but I will talk you through your orgasm. First, Kylie, I want you to make sure that your vibrator is in as far as it will go. I want it to fill you up, and once you're sure of that, I don't want you to touch it again unless I tell you to."

While he waited, she checked, pushing the sex toy in farther. He gave her time to complete the task before telling her the next instruction. "Lay down on the bed. I want you to reach up beneath the pillow."

Kylie shimmied down the bed so she could do just that.

"Beneath the pillow are a set of restraints: leather, fur-lined cuffs. I want you to grab hold of them. Keep your arms raised, and don't let them go."

She found the cuffs beneath the pillow. Where the hell had he hidden those all night?

A moment later, he spoke again. "Good girl. I bet you look so hot with that ball in your mouth. Your lips stretched around it, your tongue licking the back of it."

Her pussy clenched around the vibrator. She wished she hadn't followed his instructions and had instead put it on a higher setting.

"Not as hot as you looked with your lips wrapped around my cock, though. That was just about the sexiest thing I've ever seen. You looking up at me, your eyes filled with tears as I jammed my cock down your throat."

She moaned.

"Yeah, baby. That's exactly the noise you made. Your mouth all nice and full."

She couldn't stop herself from writhing on the bed.

"You're such a slut for me, aren't you?" He didn't give her time to answer. "Of course you are. Any man you've been with before me never did for you what I can. Never made you so wet you squirmed. Never made your nipples tight with just a glance. And yes, I saw that tonight when they beaded for me. Only for me. They're nice and tight right now, aren't they? Just begging for my mouth."

Arching, her hand loosened on the cuff.

"Don't even think about touching them."

She let out a frustrated groan, but she obeyed.

"Imagine I'm there with you. Imagine I'm blowing on them softly and then pinching them so hard you cry out."

Each word he said came to life in her mind. She could almost swear she felt him there with her, but imagination wasn't nearly enough.

"I can't wait to wrap my tongue around them. To bite one, then the other, until you scream."

Fuuuuck. Kylie's head rolled to the side. She squeezed her eyes closed. The vibrator pulsed between her legs as she let Freddie's naughty words wash over her.

"While I feast on your nipples, you'd spread your legs nice and wide for me, making plenty of room, showing me where you really want to be touched. I'd touch that hot little pussy of yours, just barely brushing it, until you were squirming and begging for me."

Her back arched off the bed.

"Not until you'd soaked the sheets would I shove three fingers in deep."

She grabbed the restraints harder in an attempt to fight off her fast-approaching orgasm.

She heard the sound of a zipper through the phone. What was he doing?

"Do you have any idea how hard you make me, Kylie? How badly I want to feel that tight little cunt squeezing me. Reach down and grab the vibrator. Fuck yourself with it. Pretend it's me."

He didn't have to tell her twice.

With her legs spread so wide her feet hung off the sides, she pulled the toy out and shoved it back in, riding it like it was his cock.

She just knew his hand was wrapped around his dick, stroking himself while she got herself off.

In and out, the toy moved, but she needed more.

"Touch your clit, Kylie. Pinch it."

With one hand, she stuffed the toy inside, and with the other, she followed his instructions. It was obscene but no less than everything else he'd had her do up until that point.

"Harder, Kylie. Harder."

Everything was becoming a blur of motion. She moaned against the gag.

"That's right, baby. Fucking make yourself come. Come all over that toy, like I want you to come all over me."

His words sent her over the edge. The gag stifled her groan, but it had no control over the tremors that wracked her body. Shaking and arching, she came hard, just like she always seemed to when Freddie was in charge.

Through the phone, she barely registered the sounds he made. He must have jerked off while she'd come, and damn, that seemed hot, but she wished she'd been able to see it instead.

Before she could remove the gag, before she could ask him any questions about the upcoming week, about how he knew her body and what she needed so damn well, his voice came over the line once more, this time sounding a bit more relaxed. "Sleep well, Kylie. I'll see you Thursday."

Chapter Nine

When Thursday came, Kylie didn't know what to do. She stood in her closet, glancing through her wardrobe. She knew she should be getting ready for work but couldn't help but think about that coming evening. Was she going to the club? What should she wear?

It was December the twenty-third, the day Freddie would make his decision.

Kylie couldn't help but think he'd already made up his mind that he was going to take her home tonight. She was already imagining him sweeping her away from the club in favor of his private dungeon, or red room, or whatever the hell he wanted to call it.

But so far, she had no real indication that would be the case.

In fact, the text she'd received that morning from an unfamiliar number had her completely confused. It had been from Conan:

> If Santa doesn't come through tonight, I expect you to text me instead. I promise to reward that pussy well.

She'd been shocked and surprised by the text. She was flattered that he'd bothered to remember her, but she wasn't at all as excited as she had been by the texts Freddie had been sending her all week.

I just jacked off in the shower thinking about how fucking hot you looked with my cock in your mouth.

On your break today, I want you to fuck yourself with two fingers and make yourself come. Think of me when you do.

I can't wait to see my handprint on that tight little ass of yours.

Each text turned her on more. She wanted to be at his mercy, but when Conan's text came through, she floundered. How did he have her number, anyway? Freddie must have given it to him, but why? Was it his way of letting her down easy? Passing her off to another man?

That couldn't be the case.

She tried to distract herself at work, but having Hannah nearby was a constant reminder. It didn't help when Hannah asked her what she planned to wear that evening.

It wasn't until her shift was coming to a close that a package was delivered. She and Hannah stole away to the break room to open it.

Inside was a blood-red rose laying atop a little black dress, with a pair of black fuck-me stilettos. The dress was classy enough but had a rather sexy edge. The hem was not quite as short as the elf costume he'd sent, but still not nearly modest enough. The halter neckline dropped into a deep, plunging V, and there was no way she could wear a bra with it. The dress was void of a back, except for several silver chains that drooped from the neck to the waistline.

"Damn, girl!" Hannah whistled. "You're going to look fine in this."

Kylie couldn't help but agree. The dress was stunning, and she couldn't wait to wear it for him.

She picked up the card that had accompanied the outfit:

My place. Tonight at 7 PM. I'll feed you first. Don't be late.

Kylie glanced at her watch. "Seven? I'm not going to make it!"

"Go now. You don't want to be late." Hannah winked at her. "Well, maybe you do."

After getting home and rushing through a shower, she blew out her hair and tossed on a bit of makeup before slipping into the dress. It fit like a dream.

She spun around a few times and found it difficult not to stare at her ass with each pass. She did look good. She was debating what to wear beneath it, but she decided to skip panties to avoid any unnecessary lines. The fabric was stretched tight enough over her ass as it was.

She was pulling on her long coat when his text came through:

> Don't forget the shoes. I want to feel them digging into my back when you come against my face later tonight.

Good thing she'd skipped panties. They'd be soaked after that message.

Halfway down the driveway, she ran into her brother. X grabbed her by the elbow. "Can we chat for a second?"

Very aware of the time, Kylie debated her answer. "Fine, but you literally have like a second."

He let go of her arm and ran his hand through his hair. Kylie sighed. It was going to be one of those talks—a tough love, big brother talk. She so didn't have time for it and was about to say as much, but then he shocked her with the topic he brought up.

He let out a breath. "I know you're screwing around with Freddie."

Kylie tried not to let her surprise show. "Janet told you?"

"No." He frowned. "I figured it out."

She thought back to all the dirty texts Freddie had sent her. There was no way X could have gotten her phone. "How?"

"At the party. You were watching him. I don't know." X put his hands into his pockets and shrugged. "It was different than how you used to look at him. Something changed. I figured you're screwing around."

"You going to warn me to stay away from him?"

He chewed his lip.

"Oh my God, you are!" She was stunned he cared. He'd never bothered to chase away his friends when they came sniffing around one of his sisters. "I can take care of myself, X. He's not going to hurt me."

"No. Actually, I'm not worried about you. I don't want you to hurt him."

"I'm sorry, but what?" Screw being late.

X sighed. "Freddie is vulnerable. More so at this time of year. I want you to be careful with him."

Vulnerable? Kylie nearly choked. The man who had threatened to spank her? Who had voluntarily given her to another man to bind, tease, and pleasure publicly? Vulnerable? Yeah, right.

"Maybe you don't know him as well as you think you do," Kylie suggested. There was no way X could know about the BDSM stuff and still think of Freddie as needing protection. From her, of all people!

"I know him pretty well, sis. He's fragile. More so at Christmas."

Kylie rolled her eyes. *Yeah, that had to be why he was at the club hunting for subs*, she thought sarcastically.

X gave her one last warning before leaving her in the driveway. "Just don't break his heart, Kylie. That's all I ask."

She was seven minutes late.

From all those naughty books she'd read, she knew she'd be punished for her tardiness, and frankly, she couldn't wait. As she stood on Freddie's stoop in her long coat, waiting for him to answer the door, she couldn't help but focus on what the night had in store for her.

Would he spank her? Would he make her go to her knees again? Would he use restraints?

He hadn't asked her to bring the cuffs or the ball gag from the weekend.

Bare beneath the dress, she rubbed her thighs together and tried to tell herself to be calm. Don't jump him when he opens the door.

He didn't keep her waiting long. The second he opened the door, she had to remind herself, *don't jump him, don't jump him, don't jump him.*

God, he was yummy. He stood tall and proud by the door in grey slacks, a plain white t-shirt, and a matching grey dinner jacket. His blond hair was styled perfectly, and his green eyes were sparkling with mischief. He didn't say a word. Instead, he let the tension build between them as he glanced over her features, coat, and the stilettos.

"I'm late." She blurted out. Instantly, she felt the blush creep across her skin. Could she be any more obvious? She may as well have asked him to spank her. To cover up, she quickly amended, "I mean, I'm sorry I'm late. X decided he wanted to have a brief, little chat before I could leave the house."

A grin brightened his face. "Come in, Kylie," he said with a laugh. When he'd shut the door behind her, he silently extended his hand, offering to take her coat.

She shrugged out of the jacket. Luckily, it was warm inside his house. She took a little peek at the entranceway and into the nearby living room. She'd never been inside his home before but had dropped X off a few times.

What she saw was a wide variety of whites and creams, from the walls to the curtains to the carpets and furniture. There were only a few splashes of color here and there, primarily pale pinks or the odd painting with some blue in it. It was sort of impersonal and cold. She couldn't imagine her brother and Freddie playing video games in front of the big flat-screen TV.

"You look beautiful," Freddie's voice whispered around her. While she'd been glancing around, he'd disposed of her coat and drew nearer.

She flushed at the compliment.

Maybe the lack of feeling she got from the brief glimpse into his home was merely because this wasn't his regular home. He spent most of his time in the south. He was the source of warmth in this house, not the items that occupied the space. He was flesh and blood. When his hand fell to the bare skin at the small of her back, it was further proof. Warmth spread through her at his touch.

"So..." she prompted.

His eyes twinkled as he glided one thumb across her lower lip. "So very eager." The hand on her back prompted her to move forward. "But dinner first."

She wanted to drop her head back and groan in aggravation, but instead, she followed him into the dining room, exercising all the patience she could muster.

"So, what did your brother want?"

"Actually, he wanted to warn me to stay away from you."

Freddie laughed.

"You don't seem surprised."

"X is smart. I'm not surprised he figured out that I'm fucking his little sister."

Kylie turned to face him. "But you're not." He kept postponing that part with silly things like food and his stupid rules.

He stepped closer, bringing his body into contact with hers. "But I will be soon, won't I? If I asked you to hop up on that table and spread your legs right now, you would, wouldn't you?"

Blushing, Kylie glanced away. She wouldn't even hesitate. "You make me sound like a whore."

His hands snaked out, grabbing her so fast she didn't have time to react. One wrapped around her hip, holding her pelvis in place against his; the other grasped her chin, forcing her to meet his gaze. "You're not a whore. You're mine. And I fucking love how badly you want me."

She stared up at him. His words were true. She did want him. She was already wet enough that she knew if he asked her to sit on the table and bare her pussy, she'd be able to take him with little to no prep. She'd never felt so primed before.

Thinking he was going to kiss her, she leaned forward the slightest bit until he completely released her, stepping aside and pulling out a chair at the long, vacant table.

Sighing, she slid into the chair before he pushed it in. He took the seat next to her at the head of the table. As he scooped salad onto two small plates, Kylie spared a quick look around.

Again, there were no photographs, just simple artwork void of much color. It was such an empty house.

Using his phone, Freddie put the radio on, filling the quiet and chasing away the loneliness. Kylie dug into the salad on her plate as soon as Freddie set it before her. Mixed spring greens, candied pecans, goat cheese, and shaved beets. She wondered if he'd made it himself, if he had a personal chef, or perhaps he'd sent for takeout.

"X surprised me, though. He seemed more worried that I would hurt you rather than being worried about me. Weird, right?"

He frowned. "Really?"

"Yeah. He called you vulnerable."

The corner of Freddie's mouth turned up as though he was amused. "What X thinks doesn't matter. What do you think?"

"Honestly?"

"No. Lie to me, Kylie. See what it gets you." His gaze twinkled.

Now she laughed. "That's not the threat you think it is."

His eyes widened slightly, and his nostrils flared. She was sure he was as affected by their chemistry as she was.

She nodded at his plate, happy to turn the game around on him. "You should eat."

He picked up his fork but told her, "You don't realize the fire you're playing with."

With a little shrug, she speared more salad onto her fork. They ate silently for a few minutes until Kylie couldn't take it anymore. "To answer your question, I don't know what to think of you anymore. You've turned my life upside down lately. You're still a really nice guy, but you're not the pushover I thought you were."

He lifted an eyebrow. "I've never been a pushover, Kylie."

"I guess I've had you pegged wrong." Kylie glanced at her plate. "I mean, there's no way you could survive in the business world without a backbone."

A smile crept onto his face. "Definitely not. You can't close million-dollar deals by letting people walk all over you. However, I do prefer to leave as much of that up to the financial and legal departments as I can. I'd rather be in development with the computer geeks."

As Freddie cleared away the salad course, Kylie said, "And you couldn't be a Dom if you were a pushover."

He paused with a dish in each hand. "You're new to the scene, but most Doms are caring and considerate. There's more to them than being bossy and..."

"Arrogant?" Kylie supplied when he faltered.

"A hell of a lot more," he told her before leaving the room and returning with two full dinner plates, each loaded with a chicken cutlet with a side of green beans and mashed potatoes. "Now, eat."

His don't-question-me tone made her grin. Arrogant, bossy, cocky, and so damn sexy, but something else snagged in her mind.

"It was really nice what you did for Hannah on Saturday. How you held her hair back, then when she was recovering, you were like, I don't know, petting her."

"I was?" His brows pinched together, but then he shrugged. "Habit, I guess."

"Is it a habit for you to pet women's heads when they're on their knees in front of you? Or is that just Hannah?"

Freddie dropped his fork, a smirk on his delicious lips. "Jealous, babe?"

Trying not to answer that, she bit her lip.

"The only woman I want on her knees in front of me is you. And I sure as hell won't be petting your head. I'll be gripping your hair nice and tight as I feed my cock down your throat."

Kylie's mouth dropped open. Uncomfortable didn't begin to

describe how wet and needy she was from his dirty words. How had she fallen into this trap again? He was so much better at this naughty game than she was.

"Put some food in that mouth before I stuff it with something else."

She snapped her jaw shut, her gaze darting from him to her plate. She still didn't have any real answers about him and Hannah. Before asking her next question, she tried to calm her racing heart and picked up her fork. If she were compliant, maybe she'd get some answers.

Several bites later, she tried again.

"I know she wanted you last year." Kylie breathed and boldly asked, "What did you do with her?"

Freddie reached for his glass of wine and took a sip. "You really want to know the dirty things I did with your friend?"

She hesitated. Did she?

"I think so. I can't stop wondering about it."

He glanced away and back again. "It's not nearly as bad as you're imagining. I wasn't really interested in her. I'd already planned on choosing Angel, and unfortunately, she'd picked up on it, which made her bratty and supercilious, so one evening, I gave my attention to Hannah instead."

Kylie put her fork down in favor of her wine glass. She needed it to steady her nerves.

"I made her sit on my lap and finger herself until she came. I never touched her pussy. I did play with her nipples a bit. Kissed her neck and such."

She took a breath. That wasn't so bad.

"The entire time she'd been trying to hook my attention, another Dom was trying to attract hers. She was oblivious to him, though. So that night I played with her, I instructed her to keep her eyes on the man at the bar. I think she came more from his stare than anything I'd done."

"Oh." She poked another piece of chicken with her fork. "Who was he?"

His tone turned cold. "The man you kept dancing with at the

club."

"Oh, her Dom. That was Darrell." Kylie continued to eat, her mind now at ease.

"Yes, well, I knew he was interested in her and found a way to connect them. She didn't vie for my attention after that night. Though I never would have bothered if I knew how much he'd enjoy having his hands on you."

Kylie's eyes widened. "It was just dancing."

His gaze bore into hers. "From the second you walked into that club, you belonged to me. No one else."

And yet he'd made her wait weeks for tonight. Anger rising, she dropped her fork. "Then why pass me off to Conan like some kind of trinket or toy? Yes, some toy you decided to share."

"Watching him touch you, watching him make you come, watching you fucking beg him for more killed me. But I needed to know you wanted this, wanted me. And I needed to know how far you were willing to go in order to get it."

Kylie swallowed. His expression had darkened, and she knew she was walking a tightrope. They stared at one another for a long moment before his jaw finally relaxed, and he sliced off another strip of chicken from his plate.

"Why did you give him my number?"

His attention was once again drawn away from his plate. "I didn't give him your number."

"Then how did he get it?"

Freddie shrugged. "He's a wealthy man, Kylie. Wealthier than me. If I wanted a woman's number, it would be a simple phone call to make that happen. No different for him."

"Oh." So Conan had tracked down her information. She wasn't sure how she felt about him having access to her private information so easily.

"What did he want?"

"He offered to take your place if you didn't choose me."

"What did he actually say? What words did he use?"

"He said that I should contact him if you didn't come through tonight. That he'd..." She trailed off, feeling awkward saying the words. Blushing, she cleared her throat. "That he'd reward my pussy well."

Oh my God, saying the words left her flushed and feeling far too vulnerable for her liking. How did Freddie speak so bluntly all the time?

Freddie's eyes narrowed, and through clenched teeth, he muttered, "And what did you say in response?"

She shrugged. "Nothing. I didn't know what to say. I assumed you'd given him my number." Glancing down at her plate, she confessed, "I thought maybe that was your way of passing me off. Maybe you were done with me."

This time, when he dropped his fork, it clattered to his plate with such force that she jumped in her seat. His hand snaked out and grabbed her wrist. "Tell me you're done eating because I'm ready for dessert."

Kylie gulped. The ferocity in his gaze was startling. She didn't know what he intended next but knew it wouldn't be laid out on a dessert plate or accompanied by coffee. And that was fine by her.

When she gave a slight nod, he rose from his chair and rounded the table. His thumb stroked the tender skin at her wrist while he hooked her chair leg with his foot and dragged it out from the table.

Cupping her chin, he stared down at her. With her heart thumping in her chest, she licked her lips and squeezed her thighs shut in a futile attempt to stop the pulsing she felt there.

"I don't think so." His laugh was wicked. His hands dropped to her knees, and he pried her legs apart as far as the tight skirt would allow. His fingers traveled up her thighs until they connected with her slick, bare lips. "This belongs to me, and only me. Conan doesn't get to see or touch it again."

His sly fingers slipped out from beneath the material and trailed upward before plunging into her top and grabbing her tit. "Or these."

Kylie moaned as his fingertip brushed over her nipple. She wanted, needed, more.

But Freddie's hand shifted away again, tracking up her body

until the pad of his index finger coasted over her lower lip. "And these lips. These beautiful dick-sucking lips belong to me."

When she sucked his finger into her mouth, she saw his eyes flare with heat.

He pulled the tip out and dragged it down her chin, leaving a wet path. Why that made her even hotter, she wasn't sure. He gripped her chin. "I want you to hike that skirt up around your hips and spread your legs wide, feet on either side of the chair."

Ready to begin, Kylie quickly complied with his request. Modesty be damned, she wanted whatever he had to give her, and when he knelt between her legs, she knew she'd made the right decision.

His thumbs coasted along her thighs, lighting her skin on fire with each inch. She shuddered as he lowered himself and buried his face between her legs. His gaze stayed glued on hers as his fingers slipped along her vulva, and his lips closed around her clitoris. Her hips bucked upward with each suck, each stroke. He dragged two fingers down to her entrance and plunged them deep inside.

One hand gripped his hair tightly, and the other clung to the edge of the chair as he ravaged her with his mouth.

"Please," she begged as she drew closer to the brink.

He lifted away and pulled her hand from his head to place it next to her on the chair. "So Kylie, should I eat this pretty little pussy until you come or keep you on the verge of orgasm instead?"

"Please," she said again, this time lifting her hips toward him.

"Please, what? Tell me what you want." His green-eyed gaze consumed her as he waited for her response.

"Let me come."

Triumph flashed across his face. "Not until you tell me that you're mine."

Gladly. "I'm yours."

His eyes narrowed. "And I can do whatever I want with you? If I want to fuck your mouth, your pussy, your ass, I can have you however I want?"

Now, she paused. He'd mentioned her ass before. Spanking she was ready for, hell, she pretty much craved that first stinging slap, but anal? Hannah swore she should try it that she'd love being so filled.

When she hesitated, he laughed and lowered his face back to her sex.

Closing her eyes, she soaked up every sensation, every touch, every lick he gave her. He brought her to the edge of orgasm only to stop. Three times he brought her to the threshold only to deny her. Finally, she was begging in earnest. "Please, Freddie, let me come."

"Who do you belong to?" his whisper was so quiet against her thigh.

She glanced down at him. "You. You. Whatever you want from me, you can have." Her body trembled and strained for the release that was just out of reach. "Just let me come."

He resumed his effort, and moments later, she was coming against his mouth, riding wave after wave of pleasure, until she fell back, limply, in the chair.

Freddie swept back up to his full height. "Now that we've had dinner and dessert, I think it's time we get onto your punishment."

Her eyes widened. "Punishment?"

"That's right, girl." He reached down and pulled her to her feet. "You were late." He cut her off when she opened her mouth to remind him of her excuse. "I gave you a time to be here, and you disobeyed. That was naughty of you. And naughty girls get punished."

"What are you going to do to me?"

"Anything I want, Kylie," he told her before tossing her over his shoulder. "Anything and everything I want."

Chapter Ten

Sending up prayers that he didn't drop her, Kylie clung to Freddie's body as he carried her down a set of stairs to his basement. He set her on her feet at the bottom. Glancing around, she was disappointed by what she saw.

Instead of some red room dungeon-type setup, all she saw was a gaming room. A billiards table was to the left, and a bar was on the right. A giant television screen took up a considerable portion of one of the walls, and the reclining sofas looked soft and inviting. This room screamed Freddie. His style and personality could be seen throughout the space. This was probably where X and Freddie gamed, but neither one had much time for that these days.

Before she could ask what they were doing, Freddie took her hand and led her through the room toward a door.

Anticipation built inside her as she watched his hand wrap around the doorknob.

This is more like it. She stepped inside the room. "I'm guessing X hasn't been in here before."

Freddie shut the door behind her. His lips brushed her ear. "If he knew about this room and all the dirty shit I plan to do to you, he wouldn't have let you leave the house."

Kylie shivered.

"What do you think?"

The big bed drew her gaze first. It was enormous, or at least it seemed that way. It was undoubtedly a king or larger, but the frame encompassing it made it all the more imposing. The headboard was a metallic grid, and four impressive posts stretched upward from each corner of the mattress. There was an abundance of space to tie someone to that bed. The red brick wall behind it only added to the atmosphere. This was a playroom, not a bedroom.

There were no nicely painted walls, no artwork. The room was brick and metal. Black and red dominated the space.

Tearing her gaze from the bed, she saw a spanking bench in one corner and a sex swing in the other. Along one wall was a large cabinet.

"Well, that bed certainly isn't for sleeping."

He chuckled. "No, it's not."

She turned to face him. "So, uhm...what kind of things are you into exactly?"

"A little late for that question, isn't it?"

"Isn't it a Dom's job to make his sub feel safe?"

"At any point, have you felt unsafe?"

"No." She hesitated. "But you've mentioned ass play a few times."

"Does that make you uncomfortable?"

"I've never..."

"Taken a cock up your ass before?" he supplied for her.

She shook her head. She had mixed feelings about the idea of anal sex, though if anyone made her feel safe enough to try, it was Freddie.

Freddie closed the distance between them with one step. "If at any point tonight you need me to slow down, you say yellow. Red is for stop. You have control over what happens to your body while you're in this room. Do you understand?"

"Yes."

"Yes, what?"

She thought for a moment before realizing what he wanted. "Yes, Sir."

His lips twitched upward for a second. "Do you feel safe?"

She nodded.

"Good. Yellow to slow down, red to stop." He brushed a strand of hair away from her face. "That said, before the night is through, I'm going to own every part of you. Your mouth, your pussy, your ass. And I will make sure you enjoy every second of it."

"I want that." Kylie wasn't sure if it was the wine with dinner or finally getting the promise of good sex, but she felt bold when she told him, "I want anything you're willing to give me."

"Then it's time for your punishment. I want you over the bench."

Kylie took a few steps toward the funny-looking piece of furniture before stopping. She'd seen a few at the club, but each one had looked different, and frankly, Freddie's seemed more elaborate than the ones at the club. "I'm not sure how it works."

Freddie passed her and approached the bench. She was surprised at how low it was. She assumed her body draped over the largest cushion, but she wasn't sure which way to lay. Pointing, he instructed her to crawl onto it, placing her forearms along the two pieces that angled upward and her legs along the ones that angled down.

While she rested against the cool leather, Freddie strapped her arms to the bench. The Velcro would ensure she couldn't move. Next, he strapped her legs down and rolled her skirt up, exposing her ass and pussy. Her legs were spread wide enough to give him complete access. It was a vulgar position, but she was wet already, and it had nothing to do with her recent orgasm. The lingering promise of a spanking had her excited. Knowing she'd be at his mercy all night had her drenched.

Slowly, his palm caressed her bare bottom. In lazy circles, he stroked, nearly lulling her with his soft touch, but when he separated her ass cheeks, she squirmed, well, squirmed as much as the restraints would allow.

His hands left her body, but one returned. He landed a hard smack to her right butt cheek.

She gasped at the sting.

"You're mine to do with as I please, so hold still, or your punishment will take even longer."

Kylie tried to hold still, but once again, he parted her cheeks. This time, his finger glided over her back entrance. Her entire body tensed.

"Relax," he whispered, but when her body failed to follow his order, he spanked her again.

Time and time again, he struck her, alternating between each cheek. Occasionally, he'd strike her outer thigh. With each hit, her passage pulsed, and wetness leaked out. Soon, she was pushing backward as much as the restraints would allow. She wanted more.

"My naughty girl likes her punishment. Maybe a little too much." He stepped away from her and approached the cabinet. Stuck facing a wall, she had no idea what he was getting, but she heard a package rip open. Her pussy clenched in anticipation.

Something cold hit the top of her ass. Lube.

His fingers slid through it, gliding down once more to her asshole. He pressed lightly against it, but even with the lube, her body warred with the idea of being penetrated there. "You won't keep me out of here, Kylie. This ass is mine, just like the rest of you."

The words made her relax a small fraction, but not enough. With his other hand, he reached down between her legs and rubbed her clit. She couldn't help the moan that escaped her lips.

"That's right, Kylie. Give it all to me. Give me everything."

Pushing into his touch as much as she could, she felt the next orgasm building. That's when his finger penetrated her virgin hole. It was just the tip, just a bit, but it felt huge and foreign and, oddly, good. Nerve endings were stimulated, and she wished she had freedom of movement to rock her hips. She needed just a little more pressure in order to get off.

But Freddie had other plans. Both hands left her, and instead, she felt something else touching her ass. When she tensed again, he landed a hard smack on her thigh. "It's a small butt plug, nothing more, Kylie."

How could he be so blasé? Nothing had gone up her ass before.

"One day, I'm going to fuck this tight little asshole, and you're going to love it, but for now, we need to work on stretching you out. Tonight, we'll start small and work our way up so that, eventually, you can take my cock. For now, though, I want to fuck your pussy with your ass full. And you're going to love it."

Each word turned her on. Sure, the dirty talk pressed all the right buttons for her, but the idea that tonight wasn't a one-time deal, the fact that he spoke about the future, even just their sexual future together, was a big turn-on.

"Okay, Kylie?"

"Yes, Sir. Please, Sir."

"You're such a good girl."

This time, when his hand returned to her clit, he increased the friction, rubbing her, dipping into her passage, pushing her closer and closer to the edge until she finally fell. As the orgasm rushed through her, he slipped the plug into her butt.

"Good fucking girl," he repeated, this time patting her ass before walking away. He completely left the room—she felt his absence immediately—but when she heard running water, she realized he would return as soon as he washed up.

She was right, though this time, when he entered her line of vision, he'd opened his pants and was stroking his cock as he came toward her.

"You look so sexy, all laid out for me, your ass red from my hand, and my plug in your butt." He jacked his cock. "Fuck, Kylie, you get me so goddamn hard."

"Freddie, please," she moaned, unsure of what she was asking for. Her gaze was glued to his dick.

"Please, what, Kylie? Please make you come again? Please fill your pussy and fuck you while you wear that plug so you come so hard you can't walk?"

She was practically panting. God, she wanted him.

"Or please shove my cock down your throat while you're helpless and bound."

Her body flushed with heat. "Oh, my God, please. Yes, please."

He moved in front of her. "Open your mouth."

Placing the head of his cock against her lips, he pressed forward as soon as she opened. At first, it was simply the tip as he eased in and out, stroking himself with just her lips and the briefest contact with her tongue. It wasn't long before he was pressing in deeper and deeper. From her position on the bench, she couldn't take all of him, but it seemed that wasn't his intent.

She felt him harden against her tongue. She tasted him when a wave of pre-cum seeped from the tip.

The way his hips bucked forward had her wanting to feel them bucking against her pelvis or her ass. She didn't care what position he took her in tonight—she just wanted him to take her.

She hadn't lied when she'd told Hannah that sex had never been good for her. Her partners had been lazy and uncaring, but with Freddie, her body felt like it was on fire. He promised she'd come hard, and she believed him.

When he pulled his cock from between her lips and stepped away, she knew she was even closer to that promised release.

He freed her hands and ankles, and though she wasn't restrained for long, he took the time to rub her muscles before instructing her to stand and face him. He'd tucked himself away and zipped his pants.

Taking hold of the hem of her dress, he said, "I want you naked." He whisked the dress up and over her head. A few of the chains from the back snagged in her hair, but he carefully liberated them before setting the dress over the bench. It wasn't the first time he'd seen her naked, but it seemed somehow more intimate this time. Her nipples had pebbled to hard points, and her body strained to be closer to him.

"Kneel."

Thinking that now he wanted to fuck her face, Kylie got on her knees, only to find he didn't order her to part her lips. He didn't even touch her. Instead, he walked away and perched on the end of the bed.

"Crawl to me."

Kylie choked. "I'm sorry. What?"

"Did I stutter?"

"No."

"I don't want to repeat myself. When we're alone, I'm in charge. You do as I say without question. If I ask you to do something, there should be no hesitation."

"But—"

"No, buts, Kylie. Now get on your hands and knees and fucking crawl to me. I want to see that ass up in the air and your tits swaying with each move you make."

Swallowing, Kylie drummed up her courage and did as she was told.

"Look at me," he commanded when she would have averted her gaze and focused on the floor.

She raised her head and focused on his face. Heat flared as she drew closer and closer. When she was directly in front of him, between his sprawled legs, he leaned down. "Kiss me, Kylie."

This time, there was no hesitation. Reaching upward, she sunk her fingers into his hair and pulled him down until his lips collided with hers. Their tongues sparred and mated. She couldn't keep her hands off him as her tongue glided against his.

It seemed she'd been waiting forever for free reign to touch him, and now that she had her chance, she wasn't going to miss out. Running her hands over his shoulders and through his hair, she found she couldn't get enough of him. His smell, his taste, his feel. He was solid everywhere she touched. He was a millionaire, business guru, artist, and Dom, yet he still found time to work out.

While she clung to him, his hands dropped down to her breasts. He flicked at her nipples simultaneously, repeating his torture until she was bucking her hips forward and clutching at his shirt.

After tearing his mouth from hers, he ordered, "Strip me so I can flip you onto this bed and fuck you senseless."

Eager for that, too, she pushed aside kissing him, and went to work on his clothing. She stripped off his jacket and pulled his shirt up over his head.

Fuck, he was fine—all hard muscle, with a slight tan to his skin. A bit of hair sprung from his chest, stretching between his pecs and trailing down his stomach. She followed that trail and went to work on his pants. First, the button, then the zipper. To help her, Freddie stood up.

When he stood as naked as she was, he instructed her to crawl up on the bed on all fours. After another trip to the cabinet, he returned with a set of wrist restraints and some rope. He secured the restraints around her wrists. They were soft against her skin.

Next, he looped the rope through the hooks on the restraints and tied it around one of the squares on the grid at the head of the bed. When she tested it, she had a bit of give but not much.

Again, he went to the cabinet. This time, she glanced over her shoulder to watch.

All he retrieved was a foil packet. He tore it open and rolled the condom down his shaft. He came to the bed and placed one leg next to hers. His dick rubbed along her labia. She arched back against him. With two fingers, he swirled around her entrance before holding her open. He fit the head of his cock against her.

"Brace your forearms on the bed. This is going to be fast."

The second she followed through with his instructions, he inched forward, filling her slowly. With the plug firmly embedded in her ass, she felt entirely too full. He was so big.

Pulling back, he dragged his cock out and pushed back in.

Within moments, he was fucking her just as he'd said—*fast*. Each stroke was hard. He angled his hips so each plunge stroked against her G-spot.

"Fuck," she muttered.

"That's right, baby. Fuckin' squeeze my cock with your tight little cunt."

"Oh, my God." Her body moved with him, and when he reached around to finger her clit, she nearly screamed. It didn't take long before she fell over the edge, her climax hitting her hard. The sensations overloaded her, her clit, her ass, her pussy.

She collapsed onto the bed. Freddie pulled out. Too spent to question it, she let her knees give way as well.

He gave her a playful swat to the behind. "I'm not done with you yet. Flip over. I want to suck your tits when I fuck you."

His words had her stirring again. She wanted that, too.

With his help, she managed to roll onto her back. The taut rope kept her arms raised above her head, stretching her out and keeping her breast lifted.

"Perfect," he said, his gaze feasted on them. "Just fucking perfect."

Once more, he was sheathed in her body, balls deep, this time with his mouth on her nipple, sucking hard.

She writhed against the sheets. Equal parts of her wanted to get away from the overload of pleasure as well as get closer to it. However, she had no control. Her bound wrists kept her where he wanted her, as thrust after thrust he fucked her.

Hard and fast, he took her, the plug constantly reminding her of how it felt to be filled and fucked by Freddie.

Another few strokes, a flick to her clitoris, and she was coming again.

"That's right, strangle my cock, baby."

"Fuck!" She couldn't hold back the scream.

Above her, Freddie roared out his climax. For the first time ever, she wished her partner hadn't bothered with the condom. She wanted to feel his hot seed pulsing into her, wanted to know what it felt like to have it drip from her body.

Maybe next time.

As her body went limp, she had only one thought. Sex would never again be the same.

Chapter Eleven

Kylie woke the next morning feeling stiff and sore in places that normally got little to no use. She could feel Freddie with every movement.

She knew the space in the bed next to her was empty, but when she opened her eyes and saw the platter with covered plates, she smiled. Tossing back the covers, she slipped from the bed and approached the tray.

The mug of coffee was still hot, so she figured he couldn't have gone far.

Throughout the night, he'd woken her twice. Once with his head between her legs and a second time with his rock-hard dick pushing against her backside.

Her female parts hadn't had such a vigorous workout in...well, in forever, and sore as she was, she hoped this breakfast would be followed by shower sex. What would it be like to have sex in the shower with a Dom?

After lifting the lid covering the first plate, her mouth watered at the smell of sausage and an omelet. The second plate contained toast. A little bowl sat on the side with assorted fruit. It was a massive meal, but clearly only for one person.

She was beginning to wonder if he'd already eaten. That's when she saw his note.

Dear Kylie,

Enjoy breakfast. Help yourself to anything in the bathroom. It should be fully stocked. There's a new outfit for you as well. Something more comfortable to go home in.

Thanks for last night. It was fun.

Freddie

Dumbfounded, Kylie stood with her mouth agape. *Fun?* It was *fun?*

What the fuck was that? It sounded like a kiss-off to her.

Ignoring the food spread out before her, she stomped naked to the bathroom. She didn't bother with a shower. Either she was sharing one with him that morning, or she'd go home and cry in her own.

Forcing herself to stop thinking he was giving her the boot, she brushed her teeth and hair and used the toilet. True to his word, a stack of clothing was next to a pile of folded towels topped with unopened shower products. The pair of grey UGG boots raised her anxiety.

He was definitely well-practiced in this. She knew he always disposed of his December twenty-third toy the next day. But she could have sworn she was different.

What had gone wrong? Had she somehow disappointed him?

Kylie instantly felt better after pulling on the panties, leggings, bra, sweater, and socks. She was no longer naked and exposed. Everything fit perfectly and felt like a warm hug. Surely, his thoughtfulness had to mean something.

And if not that, the three orgasms he'd had the night before had to mean something.

Leaving the bathroom with her boots in her hand, she bypassed the food tray and searched for Freddie.

As she descended the stairs, she noted how quiet the house had become and wondered if he was even home. Room after room, she searched with no luck until she finally came across a closed door with a beam of light emanating from beneath it. Muffled voices carried through from the other side.

There was no answer when she knocked, but she twisted the handle and let herself in since the door was unlocked.

What she found on the other side was unexpected. A projected image of a beautiful woman filled one wall. She was riding a bike and looking back over her shoulder with a teasing smile toward the camera. On a smaller bike was a little girl, her tongue sticking out between her teeth as she struggled to keep her bike upright.

Immediately, the video stopped.

"Did you need help finding your way out?"

Kylie's gaze cut to the small sofa where Freddie sat, a remote in one hand and a half-empty glass in the other. On the table before him was a bottle of Scotch.

She tore her gaze away from the bottle. "I was looking for you."

Standing, Freddie rubbed a hand beneath his eye. That's when she noticed how red they were. *From the alcohol or from something else*, she wondered.

"Well, I didn't want to be found. I hope you enjoyed breakfast, but now it's time for you to leave."

She glanced again at the video and tried to place the familiar-looking woman and child. "What are you doing?"

He set down the remote. "Look, Kylie, I don't want to be rude, but it's time for you to go."

She watched as he lifted the glass and tipped it to his lips, draining the rest of the liquid inside. "How many of those have you had?" she asked as he poured himself another. "It's not even ten in the morning."

He pinched his brow. "You need to leave."

"No." She stood firm on that point. Something terrible was happening to Freddie, and she needed to be here with him. She'd never been surer of anything in her life. "What's going on?" Her gaze once again darted to the paused video.

Freddie blocked the screen with his body as much as he could. "You need to get the fuck out of my house. Now."

Kylie couldn't help but stomp her foot. "What the hell, Freddie? You don't get to throw me out after the night we just had."

"You know what was expected—one night. None of the other girls ever dared to interrupt me. They all did as they were told. They left."

"Don't lump me in with them! What we have is more important than that."

Freddie snorted. "I needed a distraction. You provided it. Now it's over."

"What?" Kylie screeched. "You can't be serious."

"Dead serious." He winced slightly and turned his back on her in favor of the screen. That's when she realized who the woman in the video was.

His mother.

The child had been his sister.

Everything slammed into her at once. The memory of attending their funeral just days after Christmas, of him locked in a bedroom at their house over the holidays. X had cried that year; it was the first time she'd seen tears in her brother's eyes.

"They died today," she whispered to herself.

Christmas Eve, the year Freddie was seventeen. His whole family had been in the car when it was hit by a drunk driver. They'd been on their way home from shopping and had stopped to pick him up from a party. One of the kids at the party had left, too intoxicated to drive, but he'd done so anyway. The guests smoking in front of the house had heard the crash. There were no survivors; even though his sister had fallen into a coma, his aunt had had to make the devastating decision to take her off life support. That was the day Freddie had come to live with them.

Tears in her eyes, Kylie stared at Freddie's back.

His muscles seemed to tense. Over his shoulder, he told her, "You need to leave."

Shaking her head, she insisted, "No. You just want me to leave so you can drink yourself into a deep, dark hole. How is that going to help?"

"You helped enough last night. Now leave."

"No, I—"

Abruptly, he turned and stalked toward her. His gaze was hard, his face twisted in anger and hurt. "Get the fuck out."

"But—" She raised her hands to put them on his chest, but he shifted away.

"This doesn't end in some magical happily-ever-after, Kylie." The rage seeped from his gaze. "I knew I should've picked someone else. This was a mistake. You were a mistake."

Her eyes widened as she sucked in a painful breath. Here she was, falling in love with him, and he didn't want her past her usefulness to help him forget his guilt and pain.

The tears she shed moments before threatened to return, but unlike earlier, it wouldn't be a few little ones etched in sadness. No, this would be an ugly cry, full of gulps for air and swollen, red eyes. Attempting to compose herself, she sucked in a shaky breath.

How had this happen? How could she not have seen this coming? She knew his history. How had she forgotten?

Seeming to sense her sudden weakness, Freddie leaned down and caged her against the wall, placing one palm on each side of her head. The darkness in his gaze was back, and for a second, he looked more like a dangerous, snarling animal than a man as he slowly growled out his new mantra. "Get. The. Fuck. Out. Now."

Done trying to reach him, Kylie ducked beneath his arm and ran. At the front door, she flung open the closet and grabbed her coat. Not bothering to put it on, she fumbled for her keys and fled the house, leaving the black dress from the night before lying crumpled somewhere inside, along with her shredded heart.

Six days after Christmas, Freddie was supposed to fly back to the States.

Kylie had done all she could to try to forget him and the night they'd spent together. On Christmas Eve morning, she'd been a mess by the time she made it home.

She'd ignored her sister's look of pity, and when she'd run into X in the hallway, she'd given him a piece of her mind. "Worried I was going to break his heart, eh? He's fragile and vulnerable, eh? Well, fuck him, and fuck you too!"

After slamming her bedroom door, she thumped her fist against it, but neither action had proven therapeutic. She'd followed it up by crying in the shower and washing off his scent. But she couldn't do anything about the ache between her legs nor the painful pressure in her chest.

For Christmas Day, she managed to pull herself together and put on a happy face, but beneath it, she was anything but, and the following day, she'd gone back to moping.

When Saturday night came, Hannah called her to invite her to the club. At first, she refused, but eventually, Hannah had worn her down. She kept insisting that the best way to get over a guy was to get under a new one, not that that had been her plan, but the more she thought about how things had ended with Freddie, the more pissed she became.

Before getting dressed, she grabbed a bottle of Fireball from the kitchen. She sipped it straight from the bottle while styling her hair, putting on her makeup, and dressing in her sexiest outfit for the club. Armed with a plunging neckline, a short skirt, and thigh-high boots, Kylie was sure to put Freddie behind her before the night's end.

By the time she was ready to walk out the door, a plan was taking shape in her mind to help her forget about Freddie, even if she'd regret it come morning. Isn't that precisely what he'd done with her—used her as a distraction?

While waiting for an Uber, she took another swig of whiskey and sent a message to Conan. Hopefully, he wouldn't be boarding a jet tomorrow, either.

Earlier, when she'd been changing, she'd sent a photo of herself to Hannah for confirmation that her outfit was sufficient for the club. Feeling empowered by the booze and pissed at Freddie, she forwarded the image to Conan. The accompanying text read:

> Meet me at the club tonight?

She was halfway to the club when his response came through:

> You sure, babe? I thought you were with Freddie.

Kylie's eyebrows pulled down in a frown.

> Nope. It's a one-and-done kinda deal. Think you can do better?

> I'll be there. You'd better be ready for me.

Just texting the words had her grinding her teeth together. If it weren't for the whiskey, she wouldn't be letting anyone else touch her. She really only wanted Freddie. But he didn't want her.

Briefly, tears stung her eyes. No, she wouldn't cry anymore. She'd use Conan to forget.

Freddie's words came flooding back to her.

Mine.

Well, he'd discarded her. She wasn't his any fucking more.

Chapter Twelve

Arriving at the club, Kylie paid the driver and stepped out. She ditched her coat and strutted toward the bar. Some booze had taken the edge off her pain. Having more would likely be better. Besides, she needed to steel her nerves for whatever Conan had in store for her tonight.

With a whiskey sour in her hand, she turned to survey the club. She hadn't yet seen Conan or Hannah, but within a few minutes, Darrell slid up next to her and ordered a beer. "You're here early," he said.

The crowd was definitely thin at this time in the evening. She was sure it would fill up quickly, though. Most workplaces had let out a few hours ago, and many of the patrons had probably already changed and were on their way here.

"Yes, I am," she announced rather proudly. "I've got a date."

Darrell smiled at her. "Glad you hooked Santa. Honestly, I felt a little sad for the guy. Every year, it seemed as though he wouldn't make a connection with anyone, not long-term anyway. But you won him over."

Kylie shook her head, and her whole body shook with the movement, nearly causing her to spill her drink. "No, not him. Conan."

"What?"

"Yep. You're right about Santa. He is sad. And there's definitely no connection."

Frowning, Darrell lowered himself to look into her eyes. She hoped her makeup covered up any lingering redness around her eyes. "You don't really think that."

"Doesn't matter what I think." She took a long sip. "Besides, I'm not here to think."

"You sure this is a good idea? I saw him with you. He was possessive. This thing with Conan will likely—"

She held up a hand. "No offense, Darrell, but I don't need a lecture. I've warred with myself enough for now. I just want to forget, and the booze is doing a decent job at that, but Conan promised to be a better distraction."

"Fuck." Darrell ran a hand through his hair. He looked out at the club. "I see Hannah. I'll be right back."

The room began to spin a bit as she waited. Maybe she'd drunk more than she'd thought. A few minutes later, it wasn't Darrell who tapped her on the shoulder, but Hannah.

"Hey, tossing back a couple?" She nudged her.

Kylie rolled her eyes. "Darrell is a tattletale."

"Maybe." Hannah laughed. "But seriously, mixing booze and BDSM isn't cool."

"Oh, please. Can you honestly tell me you've never gotten a little tipsy and called up your Doms for a bit of fun?"

"There's a big difference between tipsy and sloppy drunk, and considering how many of those words you just slurred, I'm thinking you're the latter."

Kylie waved her away.

A giant hand fell on her shoulder. "Kylie?"

With a smile too big to be real, Kylie turned to Conan. He really was a big bastard, handsome too. Just not as attractive as Freddie.

She pushed that thought away—there was no more Freddie.

Hannah stepped in front of her. "Tonight isn't a good night."

Conan glanced from one woman to the other before presumptuously taking Kylie's drink from her. "I can see that. I spotted her the second she came in. How much did you have before you got here, love?"

Kylie threw back her head and groaned. Was nothing going to work out for her tonight? "I came here to forget and get fucked. If you won't help me with either of those things, I'll find someone else who can."

"Oh, no, you won't." Conan's big hand curled around her bicep. After asking the bartender for a water, he took the bottle in his spare hand before pulling her away. When Hannah objected, Conan explained, "You don't need to worry about your friend. I'm taking her to a private room where she can have some water and wait for Freddie." After eyeing her, he amended, "And probably throw up a bit."

She hated that he was treating her like a child who needed to be managed, but one word stood out above everything else he said. "What do you mean 'wait for Freddie'? He's not coming."

"Don't be so sure, little one. Don't be so sure."

Doing a complete one-eighty from her original thought process for the night, she announced, "I'm not going anywhere with you!"

His laugh boomed across the bar area before he reached down and hefted her over his shoulder, much like the night she met him. Before heading to the back of the club, he turned to speak with Hannah while Kylie thumped on his back, insisting that he let her go. "If it'll make you feel better, follow us, but I promise your friend is safe. I wouldn't touch another man's woman."

Not two minutes later, she found herself being placed on the floor in a private room. Conan passed her the water bottle before blocking the door with his body. It was probably a smart move, but with how the room spun, she didn't think she'd be racing for the exit anytime soon.

Hannah stood nearby with her arms crossed over her chest. "How long will Freddie be? My Doms are going to be pissed that I left the floor with you."

"They'll get over it." Conan shrugged one massive shoulder.

He glanced at Kylie. "He'll be here any minute. I called him the second you texted me for a booty call."

"You fucking bastard!"

Conan ducked when she hurled the bottle at his head. "Hey, now! It's for your own good. If I'd fucked you, Freddie never would have forgiven either of us."

"Ha!" Kylie's laugh was fake. "Well, I guess you lost out because he wouldn't have given two shits about it. He doesn't care what happens to me now."

"You couldn't be more wrong about that," Freddie's voice was quiet but firm as it carried through the room.

A tidal wave of emotions raged through her—anger, sadness, joy. She knew she'd see him again. He was too close with X for her to avoid him forever, but she never thought she'd see him so soon. "Shouldn't you be packing for your flight?"

Freddie nodded to the others in the room. "I can handle it from here."

Hannah looked unsure. Conan simply said, "You might need a puke bucket for your car."

Freddie frowned at the behemoth, then glanced at her. "You've been drinking?"

"Ironic, right?" she replied with a snort.

"Everyone out." This time, his tone wasn't so calm and collected.

Conan ushered Hannah out, closing the door behind them. Freddie crouched down to retrieve the bottle of water from the floor. "I assume this is yours? We'll take it with us."

Kylie's eyes widened. "Take it where? I'm sure as hell not going anywhere with you."

"We have a lot to discuss, and it's better done at my place."

"What, so you can toss me out on my ass again? No, thanks."

"You either come with me so we can talk, or I call your brother to come get you."

"Call him. I don't care."

Freddie's gaze dipped down her body. "You sure about that, Kylie? You really want me to call your brother and have him pick you up from a BDSM club while you've got on such a short skirt, and your tits are nearly popping out of that top?"

Kylie slapped a hand over her cleavage. "I'm not going with you."

Freddie pulled out his phone and began thumbing through it.

Running across the room, Kylie made a grab for the device. "Don't you dare!"

Quickly pocketing his cell, Freddie seized her wrist and yanked her against his chest. "Then tell me you'll come home with me. That we'll talk this out."

"There's nothing to talk out."

"Come home with me, Kylie." His words were spoken so softly that she almost missed hearing them.

Part of her wanted to go home with him, whatever the cost, but she knew it would only lead to more hurt. Right now, she couldn't handle that. "Don't call my brother."

"Then leave with me. Right now."

"No."

After a long, deep exhalation, Freddie bent down and tossed her over his shoulder. As he carried her out of the room, she thrashed against his back. She pulled his hair, she called him every dirty name she could think of, but nothing she did ended in her gaining her freedom.

For the second time that night, she was carried through the club over a man's shoulder.

For the second time that night, she slid into the backseat of a car, this time with Freddie next to her.

She sipped the water he offered, but her stomach rolled when she did. Rather than fight anymore, she rested her head against the window. She could barely focus on his words—something about a mistake.

Once more, a tear slipped out. She didn't want to hear more. She just wanted to sleep.

. . .

She woke in Freddie's bed. Like before, a tray of food sat nearby, and the rest of the bed was empty.

Sitting up, she put a hand to her throbbing head and, staring at the tray, muttered, "Fuck. Not again."

"I'd start with the Aspirin and some water."

Kylie let out a startled scream, her gaze flying to the corner of the room where Freddie sat in one of two armchairs, a sketch pad on his lap. "Oh, my God. You scared the crap out of me!"

His lips twitched up slightly. "Sorry. I thought you knew me better than that. I wouldn't leave you alone long. Not when you were so drunk."

"I don't know you at all." She frowned. "And last time I woke in this bed, you'd given me the write-off." She flung the covers off only to realize she was naked underneath. With a jerk, she tugged the sheets back up. "You stripped me!"

Rolling his eyes, Freddie set aside his paper and pencil and approached her. "Calm down, Kylie. It's not like I haven't seen you before. I didn't think you'd be very comfortable sleeping in that tight outfit you had on."

Kylie crossed her arms over her chest. She refused to thank him.

He tossed a robe toward her before turning his back on her in favor of the food tray.

Quickly, she shoved off the covers and shrugged into the robe before hopping back onto the bed. Was she going to have to do the walk of shame in her club outfit? Last time he'd given her new clothes. She doubted he would do so again today. She didn't remember much about last night, but his anger was imprinted on her mind.

He returned to the bed with a few Aspirin in one hand and a glass of water in the other. "Here."

Glowering, she reluctantly reached out to take his offering. Not taking her gaze from his, she popped the pills in her mouth and tilted the glass to her lips. Rather than move away, Freddie stepped closer and sat on the edge of the bed. "We need to talk."

"Shouldn't you be on a flight right now?"

He glanced at his watch. "In a few hours, yes. But I'm going to miss it. I've rearranged my meetings. I don't have to be back for a few more days."

"Why would you do that?"

"Because you're more important."

Her frown deepened. "I don't—"

"Hush." Freddie leaned forward and placed a finger over her lips. "I've got a lot to say, and I need you to listen." She was about to argue with that command when he said, "I'm sorry."

Puzzled, Kylie pulled his hand away. "What?"

With a sigh, Freddie pushed away from the bed. "I made a big mistake this year."

Kylie picked at an invisible hangnail to avoid eye contact. "You said that already." Tears threatened once again. Why couldn't she get over him? She'd never had this much trouble when a relationship ended.

He ran a hand through his hair. "No, that's not what I mean. I was an asshole on Christmas Eve, and for that I'm sorry."

Kylie watched him, not sure what to say. Apparently, she didn't need to say anything because he wasn't done yet.

"I was wallowing in self-pity, and guilt, and grief. Normally, my time at the club is meant as a distraction from this awful month, and the sub I pick to bring home is in complete agreement that it's only one night, and they are to leave in the morning."

"So you can get shitfaced alone."

Freddie glanced at her, but he didn't respond to her comment. "You were the ultimate distraction, but in a completely different way. Everything about you has been different, yet I treated you the same."

He began to pace. Kylie wasn't sure where his speech was going, so she opted to stay quiet.

"I've looked into getting a grief counselor. And while it's been years since I did the whole committed relationship thing, I'd like to give it a try. With you, that is."

Kylie swallowed. That was a lot to process. Questions flooded her mind, and she couldn't help but let them spill out. "How would that even work? You live in a different country. What would the sex be like? Your lifestyle? What would we tell people? Why did you wait so long to bother coming after me?" A thought occurred to her. "Is this just because I went to Conan?"

Pain flashed across his face. "Let's start with something else. We can discuss all your questions and concerns soon enough." He held out his arms. "Do you want me? Because if you don't, none of the rest of it matters."

She paused. He'd crushed her on Christmas Eve, but she'd thought of him every day since and the chance they'd missed out on. Of course she still wanted him, but she didn't want to risk her heart again. At least, she wasn't willing to do so first.

"I want you," Freddie admitted. "I loved waking up with you in my bed. I loved the way you submitted to me so completely, so beautifully. I love the way your body responds to me, but hell, Kylie, I've been half in love with you since high school. You're ballsy and confident. Gorgeous and independent. I want you in my life."

Stunned by his confession, Kylie blinked.

"And to answer some of your questions, I was planning on coming back for you. On Christmas, after my hangover cleared, I realized what an ass I'd been. I wanted to get myself organized and arrange for counseling. I need to get back home and deal with a few things, so I was going to send you some gifts and try to be back in a few weeks to smooth things over, but then I got that text from Conan and realized everything else could wait. You needed to come first and I'm sorry I didn't realize that sooner. It's been just me for so long. It's hard for me to think in terms of a 'we'."

Examining him, Kylie readjusted to sit back against the headboard. What she said next would determine their future because part of her knew if they became a 'we', her single days were a thing of the past.

"You're sure you'd want that?"

His gaze bore into her. He didn't answer but gave a single nod of his head.

The urge to kiss him was strong, but she knew her hangover

had caused wicked morning breath. She pushed off the bed and approached him anyway. Running one finger down his chest, she said, "I like the sound of 'we'." Leaning in, she kissed his pec. "But no more sharing, right?"

Freddie laughed and wrapped his arms around her. "No. No more sharing."

"We'll still go to the club sometimes?"

"Sure." He rested his chin on her head. "If you'd like, I can take you to some of the exclusive clubs down in New York."

"I'd like that." She snuggled against his chest. "What about your flight?"

"I'll go tomorrow." His fingers slipped beneath her robe. He pulled it open and dragged it down her arms. "Right now, I'm more interested in exploring this 'we' concept."

As his touch glided along her skin, she stilled his hand. "There's a lot to talk about first."

"Okay." His hand paused, but he didn't remove it. "In this area, I might need some instruction and guidance."

Kylie smiled up at him. "Well, how about you join me in the shower, and we can combine talking with, uhm...other things?"

Freddie's lips kicked up in a devilish smile. "Lead the way."

She let the robe drop entirely to the floor before grabbing his waistband and dragging his sweatpants down. Naked, with her hand in his, she pulled him toward the bathroom.

After a quick but thorough brush of her teeth, she decided talking could wait. Freddie had the water spraying before she pulled open the shower door. With a shy little smile, she stepped inside and whispered, "I'm an awfully dirty girl, will you wash me, Santa?"

Growling, Freddie yanked her toward him, his wet skin colliding with hers. "You definitely made the naughty list this year," he told her. "I'm not sure how you'll top it next year."

Epilogue

As he waited in the front hall for Kylie, Freddie chatted with Janet. "Big plans for Valentine's Day?"

"Oh yeah," she replied. "I've got the house to myself and way too much Chinese food on the way, and I think I'm going to watch *Friday the 13th*."

He grinned. "Sounds like a fun night."

"Oh yeah," she repeated absently as she fished cash out of her purse.

Since Christmas, he and Kylie had split their time between his condo in New York and their two places in Ontario. She hadn't been ready to move out of the home she shared with her siblings, but Freddie hoped that would soon change. Once she had his ring on her finger, he hoped she would move in with him. Several times, she'd mentioned wanting to redecorate his house here in Canada. She claimed it was cold and uninviting. He supposed she was right. His place in New York was much warmer.

If she said yes to his proposal in a few weeks' time, then perhaps she'd feel more comfortable using his money to redecorate. He'd purposely left the engagement ring at home because he knew he'd pop the question tonight if he had it with him. He didn't want to be cliché, proposing on Valentine's Day, so instead, he'd planned an elaborate evening for their first night back in New York.

He and Janet continued to talk while Kylie took her time upstairs getting ready. They were just going for dinner and then out to the club, but he'd given her specific instructions on what to wear—something appropriate for dinner but sexy enough for the club.

When the delivery man arrived, Freddie insisted on paying for Janet's dinner. Even though she seemed content to be home alone on Valentine's Day, Freddie wasn't sure he was buying it.

He had a sneaking suspicion about Janet. Between her eavesdropping and her snooping, along with her job as a photographer, he had a gut feeling about the types of things she was into.

After a glance at the stairs told him Kylie still wasn't ready, Freddie took a risk. "Janet?"

"Hmm?" She put away her money after leaving her bag of Chinese on the chair in the entranceway.

"I have some friends that are into some interesting things." When she gave him a confused look, he knew he'd already butchered this. "I'm just going to be blunt, okay?"

She gave a nervous little laugh. "O-kay..."

"Friends of mine are interested in getting some boudoir photographs done. They're into some kinky shit, though. But they're looking for a talented professional who can keep things confidential."

Janet's eyes went wide, but she nodded. "I can do that!"

Her eager response made Freddie think he'd pegged her right. "Great. I'll pass your contact information along to them."

She probably didn't realize it, but she'd begun using her thumb to stroke her wrist. Her pupils had dilated, and her breathing had become just a little faster. Yes, he was right, she was definitely eager. She liked to watch.

As far as he was concerned, Janet was a workaholic, and he should know since he'd buried himself in work after the death of his family, first with school, then his business. Janet needed to learn how to loosen up and have a little fun. Maybe photographing some of the couples from the club would help. He knew of several couples who wanted to immortalize their activities through tasteful photography.

"Uhm, thanks." She picked up her dinner. "I could use the extra money."

"Well, this should help. The Dom is loaded."

Janet stumbled on her way out of the front hall. "*Dom*?"

"Yep. Discretion is key in this job, but it will pay very well."

Her mouth hung open slightly. "Uh, great," she muttered before racing from the room.

Shortly after Janet's disappearing act, Kylie came down the stairs. Her halter top dress showed off a tantalizing amount of cleavage, and the skirt was loose enough that he'd be able to get his hand up it easily once they reached the club. Maybe even during dinner—maybe the car.

Freddie attempted to swallow his lust.

The day after Kylie had drunkenly thrown herself at Conan, she and Freddie had talked through the more difficult points of what their relationship would be like. They each traveled back and forth, and on the days they couldn't be together, they used FaceTime.

While Kylie had kept her job at the gym, they'd been talking more and more about the future—having kids, raising a family, and, ultimately, where they would live. It made the most sense for them to live in the States and travel north several times a year to visit her family. Kylie had been talking about returning to school and, more recently, had been spit-balling an idea of starting a charity that ensured poverty-stricken areas had hot meals for students.

He wanted Kylie to be happy with whatever path she chose, and luckily for him, he had the means to make it happen.

"How do I look?" She spun in a circle.

Pulling her against him, he pressed his lips to hers. "Fantastic."

With a grin, she dislodged herself from his hold and fetched her coat from the closet.

Two weeks ago, while cuddling first thing in the morning,

she'd told him she loved him. He'd said it to her after the first time he'd fucked her in the shower. Her hair had been dripping wet, and she was still hungover, but he couldn't wait. It had just slipped out.

Tonight, as they walked out the door, he kissed her the second they set foot in the frigid February air. His forehead rested against hers, and the words just slipped out, ruining all of his plans. "Marry me."

Kylie glanced up at him from behind mascara-covered lashes. Her lips were lush, and her expression was pure bliss as she uttered the two most important words of his life, "Yes, Santa."

Bonus Materials & Excerpts

Enjoy this excerpt from *Naughty Secret* (previously entitled *Her Naughty Secret*)

She followed Alexis down the hallway, her camera hanging from her neck.

How all these models could walk with such a sexy strut, she'd never know. Her gaze was glued to Alexis's ass. She was all but naked in the skimpy little string bikini Joshua had wanted her to wear. Janet sighed. What would it be like to be that comfortable in your own skin?

Emmett stood in the doorway of her office, smiling like the cat who'd eaten the canary. It unnerved her. But then, most things Emmett did unsettled her. She couldn't help but be ultra-aware of him. He oozed sexy. Built like a Hollywood stunt performer, with broad shoulders and narrow hips, he had sculpted muscles and a sinner's smile. He was bold and striking. Everything she wasn't.

His fixation on her was getting harder and harder to put off. Really, what could one night in his bed hurt?

Janet returned his smile with a friendly version of her own.

She knew it could hurt everything. She needed their friendship. He might not realize it, but she looked forward to conversing with him and enjoyed bouncing ideas off him, whether they were for business or art or even what type of cheese dip she should make for her annual holiday party. She looked forward to his opinions.

She especially looked forward to the times they hung out together. A few times, they'd gone to ball games or exhibits. Each time, he tried to turn it into the date he so badly coveted, and every time, she'd squashed his expectations.

Was it wicked of her? Probably. Was it self-centered and self-serving? Absolutely. Who wouldn't want the attention of a man like Emmett? It was a huge ego boost, and she was beyond flattered, but she knew if she slept with him, it would be over.

He was in it for the chase. And what did she do? She continued to run.

She stumbled a bit as she neared him. Alexis carried right on past him without a word. Odd, considering they'd be fucking later tonight, though maybe that was all it was. Emmett hadn't even bothered to look at Alexis as she passed. His gaze was glued to her.

Before she reached the doorway, Emmett straightened. "I'm going to ask you one more time, Janet. Will you go out with me?"

Janet grinned at his wording. One more time. Yeah, right. It was always the last time when it came to his shameless begging, but before she could reply, he continued.

"I could take you out to a nice dinner. Wine and dine you."

With sympathy, she tilted her head. "For the last time." She couldn't keep the flirty tone at bay when she added, "No, Emmett."

Pulling the camera strap over her head, she turned the corner into her office and froze. Her black binder was on the desk, and her top drawer was open just a bit.

She knew all the pages in the binder well, but it was flipped open to one of her favorites, a collection of images of a woman tied up and being penetrated by two big men, one buried deep inside her, the other fucking her mouth.

Shock and arousal held her still as she stared at the book. How could this have happened?

She felt his heat against her back as he approached and slipped one hand around her waist. His lips skimmed her ear as he whispered, "I'd offer to take you on a nice date, but somehow, I don't think you'd find it all that appealing."

Shame, panic, and betrayal all volleyed for her attention. She settled on betrayal. Turning, she pushed against his hold. "My desk was locked. How dare you go through my things?" Oh God, had he found the vibrator in her purse?

He didn't bother to deny it, just smiled smugly.

Through clenched teeth, she said, "So what now, Emmett? Do you think this means anything? You think what? That because you've seen some pictures that...what...I'll go out with you?"

Was that his game? Blackmail her into a date—into his bed?

Briefly, she thought about the people in those pictures. She'd signed non-disclosure agreements to protect their privacy. She'd violated that agreement the moment she'd printed their pictures for herself.

She'd been hired to take boudoir photos of a few local Doms and their subs. Each one would be protected by their lawyers. They were wealthy, so they'd ensure Emmett didn't talk. But her? They could fire her.

When Emmett remained silent, she tried a different route. She placed her camera in the center of the desk before closing the binder. "They're images for a client. Nothing more."

This time, his smile grew. "Oh, they're more all right." He advanced, the space between them gobbled up with his long, easy strides. "It may have started as a job, but those"—he pointed to the binder—"those are your private collection."

Janet tried and failed to keep her composure. When his hand took hold of her jaw, she stood immobile, barely daring to breathe as he revealed her secret. "You get off to those pictures. I'm willing to bet you have more at home." He leaned closer, his spicy aftershave enveloping her. "Tell me, do you go to the bathroom when you need to take care of things, or do you sit right there in that chair, hike up your skirt and play with that tight little pussy you keep denying me?"

Her cheeks lit with heat. Closing her eyes, she swallowed. He was so right, and she doubted she could convincingly deny it. Hell, sometimes she used pictures of him.

Flicking her eyes open, she stared at him, unsure of what to say.

He chuckled, his grasp on her chin tightening. "I've been going about this all wrong this entire time. You don't want a nice dinner date and flowers and all that crap. That doesn't get a girl like you in the mood."

Relief coursed through her. He thought she was into BDSM.

She couldn't hold in her laughter. "Yeah, I don't get off on all that spanking and being a naughty girl shit. I don't need some bad-ass Dom, so you can just back that train of thought up right now."

But Emmett didn't relent. No, his stubborn smile grew even more, flashing those damn sexy dimples. "Oh, I know that's not it, my little peeping Tom."

Her ease vanished. Shit. He *had* figured it out.

"Now, I could ask you out again, offer all the things I have before, but we both know that's not going to work." He dropped his hand, letting his fingers skim down the side of her body. "I'm going to text you my address." Those long fingers curled around her hip and pulled her against his hard body. "Then, I'm going to take Alexis home with me and fuck her in my bedroom."

High heels clicked in the hallway as Alexis returned from the change room.

His nose skimmed along her cheek, but that wasn't what caused her to gasp. His following words ripped that sound from her throat. "I'll leave the curtains open."

He stepped away seconds before Alexis stopped in the doorway. "You ready to go?"

"Sure thing." His gaze swung to Alexis before he headed in that direction.

She gave a little wave before pulling her phone from her back pocket. "Thanks, Janet. See you soon."

All Janet could manage was a tight nod, but Alexis was already gone.

Emmett stopped in the doorframe. "Tonight, Janet. I promise

not to disappoint." With a wink, he disappeared, leaving her to wonder how her world had just gotten flipped upside down.

Sign up for my newsletter for updates about the release of *Naughty Secret*!

Now, please enjoy this excerpt from *My Mistletoe Master*.

Three years later...

Low keening moans and sharp slaps came from the speakers on her tablet.

Alone yet subtly embarrassed in her parents' big house, she turned the volume down just a touch.

With her dad at work and her mother and brother recently gone to finish their holiday shopping, the welcome home from university hadn't been as momentous as she'd expected. She'd been absent for three years, barely coming home between semesters. She had thought some sort of conversation would have at least occurred, not the quick 'hi' and 'bye' as her family fled the house she had received.

It was a busy time, especially with her parents' annual holiday party. Besides, they hadn't expected her home until late afternoon anyway, so who could fault them for rushing out the door as soon as she'd arrived?

Having dumped her stuff in the foyer, she'd proceeded to make herself a cup of tea, then had settled on the couch to check her grades.

No updates.

After scrolling social media, she'd given up trying to find a distraction and, instead, pulled up one of her favorite softcore porn videos. This one featured a Dom, clad in black leather pants and nothing else as he restrained a woman. He raised one arm, then the other, locking them in place above her head with cuffs. Suspended from the ceiling, the man went about binding the woman's feet to the floor. Naked and spread eagle, she moaned for him. As he slowly raked his hand over her exposed ass, he denied her any form of release.

Growing wet between her legs, Amelia realized it had been too long since she'd had a man. Her body strained for more than her simple touch, but since she and her boyfriend had split two months ago, she would have to make do. To heighten her pleasure, she resisted her own needs, merely watching the two on the screen.

Pressing her palm against her jean-covered crotch, she watched as the woman cried out in a mix of pain and pleasure as the man repeatedly spanked her. Moaning aloud with the video, Amelia abandoned her restraint, rocking against her hand. Her eyes drifted shut as she tugged on the button of her jeans, eager to touch herself and work herself toward climax.

A cough sounded behind her, and she froze. "What a great way to start my morning."

Amelia squeezed her eyes shut. *No. No. No.*

"Please, Sir," the woman's voice rang out from the tablet.

Wide-eyed, Amelia scrambled to shut the device off, finally muting the sound and flipping the cover over the screen.

A key in the front door *that* she would have heard, but another person already in the house? Damn it!

For a humiliating minute, Amelia prayed the floor would open up and swallow her whole. After three long years, this was not how she had hoped to face him for the first time.

Frankly, she had planned to wear something sexy and elegant, and she wouldn't have acknowledged his existence either. Instead, this was wat Fate had in store.

Fuck my life.

Clutching her tablet to her chest, Amelia gathered what was left of her courage, standing to face him.

Nick Fuller. Her brother's best friend and the man she'd been miserably in love with for decades.

From behind her makeshift shield, she studied him. He still took her breath away, even after he'd destroyed her fragile heart. With an unwavering stance, he stood with sleep-tousled hair, wearing nothing but pajama bottoms, and blocked her escape. His chest was broad, his stomach chiseled, and his arms corded with long, lean muscles. His expression was dark and confused.

She realized he was waiting for an explanation. Rather than provide one, she led with, "What the hell are you doing here?"

He blinked. "I'm here for the holidays, like every year."

Amelia groaned. "My mom didn't tell me you were here yet," she admitted lamely, as though that explained her sinful behavior. Granted, her mother had barely said two words to her when she arrived.

"Three days."

At a standstill, they simply stared each other down. His gaze was curious as it examined her. Her cheeks heated.

How long was he standing there watching me?

Rounding the couch, she wondered how many days she could hide in her room before her parents dragged her out forcibly. With a bit of luck, she could avoid him at least for a few days.

But that was the coward's way out and she knew it. This year's plan had centered on pride and confidence, no matter how much she had to fake it.

I guess that plan is out the window now.

Aiming to shoulder her way past him so she could get to the stairs, Amelia put on a brave face and stalked toward him. His big body didn't budge as she tried to maneuver around him.

Attempting to edge by, she mumbled, "Maybe we could just forget about this. You know, pretend I'm just not here yet." She tried for a bright smile, but it faded when she saw humor light his gaze. Growing up, he and Gabe had teased her endlessly, and now she'd handed him ammunition.

"I don't think so," he took a step closer.

She had to tilt her head to keep his gaze. Rascal that he was, he dared to smile at her discomfort. Her body was primed for the orgasm she'd denied herself and his nearness didn't help matters. Masculinity and dominance rolled off him in waves. People had always taken notice when he entered a room. He wasn't the broad and bulky type like her brother; he was lean with a natural grace that made women think: *stamina.*

"I can't believe it. I would never have thought Gabe's little sister was such a perv."

Convinced he was merely trying to get a rise out of her, her eyes narrowed, and her determination to sock him grew. Casual as you please, she shrugged. "It's just a little kink."

His smile widened.

She knew better than to trust *that* smile.

"You're not going to tell anyone." She winced when her words sounded more like a plea than an order.

"What's my silence worth to you?"

This was the Nick she remembered from her childhood. Rebel, tease...*scoundrel*.

She ground her teeth and insisted, "You *won't* tell."

"Well, that depends on you, sweetheart," he whispered. And was it her imagination, or had he gotten closer?

Her tone matched his when she replied, "What do you want?"

Nick lifted his arm and clasped her chin between his fingers. Torn between pulling away or stepping closer, she merely stared up at him in fascination. Her lips parted involuntarily when he stroked the pad of his thumb across her lower lip.

His hand dropped when a key turning in the lock echoed through the entranceway. Amelia jumped away, fearful of being caught in yet another compromising moment.

A second later, her mom waltzed in, all business, with Gabe hot on her heels. "I can't believe you forgot your wallet."

Her brother shrugged.

"Gabe, we're going Christmas shopping. You need your wallet. Oh, Nick, good, you're up," her mom said when she noticed them in the living room. "Did you want to join us?"

He expelled a pent-up breath and smiled, though Amelia noticed a distinct sag in his usually straight shoulders. "Yeah, just give me a few minutes to get changed."

As quietly as he had emerged, Nick disappeared back down the door that led to the basement.

"Are you sure you don't want to come with us," her mother asked. She'd asked the same thing when they'd passed each other in the hallway when she'd first arrived home. Then, she'd barely gotten in the door. Now, she could go with them, but the idea of sitting awkwardly in the car so near to Nick turned her stomach. She needed to regroup.

She nodded a little too fast. "I'm sure."

"Come on, Gabe. Let's get a move on! I'm meeting Samantha in twenty minutes," her mother called up the stairs. Sighing, she stepped closer to Amelia. "I'm sorry. This wasn't the reception I had in mind, but I wasn't expecting you until this evening. We'll find time tonight, just you and me, and catch up?"

"Of course." She glanced at the boxes piled in the front hall. "Maybe I can help you with party favors over hot chocolate?"

Her mother smiled. "Sounds great." Turning to the stairs, she shouted once more for her son.

Gabe and Nick seemed to materialize at the same time.

Nick's rapid transformation amazed Amelia. Gone was his bedhead. And he'd replaced his pajamas with dark wash jeans and a black t-shirt that stretched to its limits over his muscled chest.

Gabe vanished out the door after their mom, but Nick lingered, slipping on his running shoes. "Don't worry, Amelia. I won't say a word. But you can bet I'll be back to collect."

She frowned. "Collect what?"

His grin was wicked. "My payment for my silence about your little masturbation session."

She wasn't sure what part of his sentence to focus on. Swallowing, she managed to squeak, "*Payment?*"

He winked. "You're not the only one with fantasies."

The door shut between them before she could gather her wits.

What the hell just happened?

About the Author

Romance author Cameron Allie grew up in a small town north of Toronto. As a child she loved stories, and after reading her first romance novel at age fifteen, her dreams of writing became singularly focused on the love story. She is currently living in Ontario with her husband, two daughters and with her cat, who is constantly trying to interrupt the writing process.

For updates on new releases, sales and more, follow Cameron!

www.cameronallie.com
Newsletter signup - https://bookhip.com/MTKDAAJ

f facebook.com/Cameron-Allie-180823822269814

instagram.com/cameronalliewrites

BB bookbub.com/authors/cameron-allie

Also by Cameron Allie

Paranormal Romance Stories
Pack Trouble Series

Drew

Callum

The Clayridge Chronicles

Love Spells, Full Moons and Silver Bullets

The Siren and the Water Witch

The Siren and the Hellhound

Blood Lust & Black Magic

Contemporary Stories

Love Me or Leave Me Boxset

Unexpected Changes Series:

My Mistletoe Master

Not His Type

The Perfect Fix

Somewhere to Belong

Unexpected Bliss

The Naughty or Nice Series:

Naughty List

Her Naughty Secret

Anthologies:

Holiday Hearts

www.ingramcontent.com/pod-product-compliance
Lightning Source LLC
Chambersburg PA
CBHW031313280626
47169CB00018B/1261